Also by Barbara J. Wells

Knife in the Sugar – feature length screenplay, thriller; screenwriter

10,000 Years from the Year 2000 – futuristic play; playwright

Copy Cat Capers, a trilogy – participatory children's plays; playwright

Ring of Songs – collection of eclectic lyrics; lyricist

Mammy, Jezebel, and Sapphire – modern dance story; librettist

Rag Doll – musical; librettist

Be Careful of What You Wish 4

Barbara J. Wells

iUniverse, Inc.
New York   Bloomington

This is a work of fiction. All of the characters, names, incidents, organizations, and dialogue in this novel are either the products of the author's imagination or are used fictitiously.

iUniverse books may be ordered through booksellers or by contacting:

iUniverse
1663 Liberty Drive
Bloomington, IN 47403
www.iuniverse.com
1-800-Authors (1-800-288-4677)

ISBN: 978-1-4401-4987-0 (sc)
ISBN: 978-1-4401-4988-7 (ebook)

Printed in the United States of America

iUniverse rev. date: 07/06/2009

(Back-in-the day) to friends who supported the notion of writing an African-American lesbian mystery novel, thanks: Donna Wojtczak, my wordsmith and backer for Jean Adams; Vanessa Davis for believing that music and novels go together and for not dying on your motorcycle on LSD that day in 1989; Vernita Gray for that talk one night on Halsted about the tragic legacy violence creates; Pat McCombs for that advice in your bar on Clark about keeping the story sexual with a lil' somethin' somethin' intellectual; poet Minnie Carey for irritating the *Fornicate Under the Consent of the King* out of me to agitate all things including mystery novels with human rights politics; Marilyn Boehm, my oldest fan, for bartenders/ cheerleaders Kathy Edens, Deborah Ray Steward, and the Lady Bug where the first chapter was written; for the confident promise made on Halsted, when I asked for freedom in Chicago to write without retribution openly in-your-face gay stuff, well done, Rick Garcia for this project is partially supported by a Community Arts Assistance Program grant from the City of Chicago Department of Cultural Affairs and the Illinois Arts Council, a state agency which would not have been possible back in the day when you made that promise. Special thanks to Dan Decker, Joe Plummer, and Laura Walls. Sunny Harnett and Scott Burhoe thank you for babysitting me through the process and for food, drink, and Da Band.

A portion of proceeds from sales of book and CD will be donated to Pow-Wow inc.

Author's photo by Vivian J. Williford.

1

"Condemnment one: Doors open and doors close." Satan threatened, smiling benevolently at his human mentor as they squatted upon hell's quicksand on the rim of a black hole.

"Your every condemnment is a test of my worthiness to sit at your left side for if I might be granted a wish I would never wish to be a minion."

2

It was the quickly enveloping fog that stealthily smothered the young man's sense of orientation in the deep forest, which buffered the night's silence, slathered dew on coppery breezes rank with the odor of fresh blood that hid defoliated tree tops to conceal their autumnal nakedness.

The woods ducked behind white shades that lowered in dense disguise.

A child's terrified shrills for help split the air and his eardrums.

The young man, his imagination in flight stammered, "Sh... shit!" No mistaking the fog. Over a decade had passed since the last time the pricks of stunted souls punctured his pre-pubescent spirit for the last time. The last time fog became his shroud it raised him on the other side of the day with his face turned up to yellow sunlight.

Ten years ago.

As the thought went through his mind a scene from his past played. He heard himself begging God for help. God never happened. Nobody ever came except those men. A decade ago the fog had been a savior to him. Now it threatened to bury him.

In a spontaneous moment wedged between rage and bravado the young man seized upon the decision to rescue the child. Just as quickly his flashlight beam introduced reality: fog up to his knees. He couldn't see the end of his outstretched hands. The saliva in his mouth turned to starch. Unidentifiable at first, a sharp sound pricked the air.

Twigs snapping.

The man flash-froze where he stood. His useless flashlight slid from his sweaty palm to the ground and extinguished. A twitch broke and ran along the walnut contours of his African-American features.

In the worst way he needed to believe that the child's screams resulted from Halloween antics. Yet, the brain that had delivered him from abusive foster homes and opened doors to an opera career as a countertenor that brain refused to pretend.

Not two miles south of Possum Woods—where his feet seemed encased in dry ice—waited a claustrophobic studio apartment from which he routinely escaped to walk off hours of vocal practice. The forest had always been safe. He loved being in it at night when nobody else was around. It was the only spacious solitude he could afford in Chicago.

Tomorrow he would escape for good on his first European tour. He planned never to return to the US of A where singing opera while black was a disadvantage in advancing his career.

"You there?" A taunting high-pitched voice shuttered the young man's past. He gave up any thoughts of rescue. His feet kicked into flight. Like a blind man unfamiliar with a room, he groped his way arms flailing, his heart banging quick *thu-thumps*. And like a rake over wet grass, a useless thought seized his brain. *God, help me.*

He stumbled to his knees over undergrowth. Squishy decomposing leaves stuck to the palms of his hands. He righted himself as quickly as he hit the ground. Sobered by the fall he regained his manhood. His spine stiffened.

No way would he abandon that child. The vow he took ten years ago wouldn't let him. From the closet of his childhood he viewed bloodstains on a grimy twin mattress moments before he lurched out and cut the monster.

"Never again!" He yelled feeling his way in the direction from which the scream had come, the twelve-year-old child within him, still abused, sobbed between gulps of air as he tiptoed by the sagging mattress, the nearly detached manhood, to the window, eased the creaky thing open and slid into his future under the cover of fog.

Twigs snapped.

The sound came from behind him, over his right shoulder.

The night had taken on an ominous personality smug with the rotting odor of sodden autumn leaves. Visibility remained limited, less than a foot, yet someone followed him.

"Fuck!"

Twigs snapped.

Too close.

So close that he felt evil's intent. Helter-skelter the muted countertenor lurched through bellowing fog oblivious to past vows, oblivious to tree branches that slapped and clawed his face.

Twigs snapped.

Over there.

It came as no surprise when he *thwacked* his head against a fat maple tree trunk. A trillionth of a second later a bullet gouged splinters from the tree where his head had been. Terror in his eyes reflected death glaring back at him pissed.

In a delayed reaction his common sense jumped to his defense: the shooter had night goggles. The young man flattened himself on the forest floor. He crawled. Crawled like he did that terrible night in Fallujah. Crawled until he felt tire tracks under his hands. Gasoline primed the air. He smelled his broken down ride.

The prey cocked his head side-to-side. Listened. His musician ears heard the disturbing sound of silence. With both hands he hastily wiped out the tire tracks. Blindly, he wrote in the dirt. As he did a patch opened up in the fog and delivered his beacon of hope, a red Volkswagen. The prey ran for it. He slid behind the steering wheel, simultaneously squeezing shut his eyes as he turned the key in the ignition and willed it to catch. Instinct popped his eyes open in time to see the last thing he would ever see: a bullet strangely hypnotic opened a third eye between his God-given eyes.

The door slammed on Justin Banks.

3

The abbreviated autumn day had shivered until its night turned opaque. The oppressive humidity had the effect of raising the pressure on JP to satisfy his need, instead, he butt-slapped on the salted rim of hell. Hold the lime.

In case somebody had heard the gunshots he decided it expedient to get his butt out of the woods. As he gazed down on an almond-eyed girl lying under a stately evergreen JP considered his options: kill her now, or kill her later the right way. He ran a hand down his long clean-shaved face, clicked off the lamp attached to his skullcap. The beam had done little to penetrate the layers of wet gauze.

The girl screamed.

With one hand he covered her mouth; with the other he slid a plastic pint size bottle from a black duffel bag. "You'll be quiet, now, Cindy." He poured the bottle's contents on a paper towel and applied it to her face. The squirming girl succumbed to sweet ether. He placed her in the duffel bag, snatched it up, and slung it over his shoulder.

A minute later JP checked the Global Positioning System (GPS) that he wore on his left wrist. After getting his bearings he broke off a tree branch to use as a prod as he made his way through the soup.

Fortunately, for JP the little girl was the poster child of malnutrition. Crack-addicted single mothers like Cindy's were the wombs from which he delivered his victims. Sometimes, like now, he fantasized how life would soon be. His exploits being featured on TV crime shows. Maybe even a movie. As with the real cops and reporters, the writers would say he chose tragically dysfunctional families because nobody cared.

He sneered. They'd get that wrong. It made him wonder how many other motivations they got wrong on those real crime rip-off TV shows.

He wondered if the new task force that the Chicago Police Department formed to catch serials was stupid enough to think they could profile him into custody like on TV. The idea of it made him giggle as he moved along prodding the ground while wondering where it went and where the unpredicted fog got off fucking with his agenda. Because of it the skinny man had snuck up on JP. But for that he wouldn't be running.

As his size eight boots picked their way around bushes and trees, JP's unquenched needs threatened to overwhelm his natural instinct to get the hell out of dodge. The bulge in his pants urged him to stop running and do what he came to do, what he'd planned two weeks to do.

"Two go'damn weeks, mothafucka!"

The package and carrier forged ahead. The glow-in-the-dark (GPS) directed him to his exit. Just in time, he ducked to avoid a branch wicked enough to decapitate him. He flicked on the hat light. Mostly, it flattened out against a curtain of rolling mist.

The man took his time out of fear of imprisonment, which far exceeded his fear of death. Entrenched in a childhood nurtured in slavery, his fear taught him to take well thought out steps. He took them now in spite of compelling urges to be a free madman.

Besides, the best was yet to come. He had big plans, plans twenty years in the making. Jail would end all of that.

The lumpy figure slipping through the misty woods, forced to wait until he felt safe to go into the woods again, in a fight to control his desires, reached in his duffel bag for a familiar tonic, better than gin.

4

Across town from Possum Woods in another forest preserve draped in fog—blue emergency lights flickered, red bar lights swirled, yellow lights pulsed in counterpoint to strobbing grill lights. Lead by the coroner's van, engines idled mournfully. Solemn voices talked scenarios.

A half-mile deep into Schiller Forest Preserve Lindsey-Smith's stomach tightened around an undigested sushi dinner as she watched the distant emergency lights smear a rainbow across the night's white belly. It sucked.

"I shouldn't be here." She mumbled to herself as she looked down at her feet and didn't see them. It unsettled her. The ground beneath her barely felt solid. Shivers ran from her hair to her toenails not because of the seasonal chill. "God, I hate the woods." She scratched at imaginary bugs. Crawly things lived in the forest. She needed to be someplace else, preferably a world away from the skeletal remains that lay by degrees nearby.

In the clearing where she stood, not much of it visible in the gloom, the slender woman sensed tall trees, at least five stories high. She sensed a presence that trees should not have. She had one word for it, *doom*. Her erect posture collapsed when her root beer eyes fell on a group of special task force officers; their bodies struck rigid silhouettes against a cotton candy backdrop.

"That aint right." She uttered under her breath, suddenly desperate to get the hell up out of there. Instead, giving into morbid curiosity, she listened.

"She's probably seven." A disembodied woman's voice

floated across to Lindsey-Smith from beyond the cluster of officers. She detected a Mexican-American accent.

"The 7s Killer?" Lindsey-Smith blurted out, her smoky voice cracking like a pubescent boy's. She cleared her throat, wishing she could stuff the words back in her big fat mouth.

Ten seconds later, a flashlight beam danced in her face. She realized someone had stepped out of the soup. The beam lowered to reveal a vertically challenged woman running a hand through a thicket of red hair.

"Lose the mask, Lone Ranger! This is a crime scene not a Halloween party." The sobering voice commanded and Lindsey-Smith obeyed stuffing her rhinestone mask into a black leather coat pocket. The shocking pink .9mm strapped to her hip was real. Only she knew that. Even so she felt queasy when the woman's stormy green eyes lingered on it a second too long. "A pink gun." The voice mocked. "Even play guns shouldn't be pink. Who are you, anyway? Why are you here?" She smiled benevolently. Lindsey-Smith didn't fall for it.

"Excuse me?" Lindsey-Smith asked stupidly. Her lanky body bent into a question mark. Relief arrived a long second later in the form of Lieutenant Kyniska Lake who stuck her bronze sinewy body between the two women and made the introductions.

"Lindsey-Smith Chief Boggs, head of the Special Task Force Department. Chief, we were on our way to the Rainbow Halloween Charity Ball when I got the call."

"So you bring her with you. Humph!" Boggs turned to Lindsey-Smith, "Ms Smith, where'd you get the name 7s Killer?"

"I…Guess I made it up. It's what I do. I'm a writer." Lindsey-Smith answered, confusion twisting up her face.

"Make sure I don't hear it again. In fact, I'd better not hear a word of what's happened here. Do you pick up what I'm puttin down?"

Lindsey-Smith nodded her head. She's pushier than Lake said. Eyes are stormier, too.

"She understands, Chief." Lake interjected. "We had that discussion."

Chief Boggs stepped back as if seeing Lake for the first time. "Let me guess. You're some kind of cat."

Lake smiled tightly, "Panther." She adjusted the waistband on her black tights. "I lost the whiskers...," she gestured towards the forest, "...out there somewhere."

"Perrr-fect! Bring me the bitch who should be missin that baby, Lieu." Boggs drew a hand through her crimson wicket. "I made you lead investigator because I expect you to make things happen. Who is she?" She flashed a smile at Lindsey-Smith.

Lindsey-Smith blinked away the smile and found a brain cell to grapple with Boggs. Who was she talking about, the dead girl or her? What the hell was Boggs smiling about? Maybe that was a grimace. That's it. Of course that's it. Murdered children don't bring smiles to cops' faces. Lake glared at her date then turned to the remains.

"I don't believe that girl left the world unnoticed, Chief." Lake snapped.

"Take all the resources you need." Boggs said, her eyes surveying Lindsey-Smith who in turn, to avoid trouble, cast her eyes on Lake.

The whole thing felt strange to Lindsey-Smith, because Lake had turned off her sensuous let's play persona and replaced it with edgy and dangerous the instant the call came in about a child's body in the woods. Lake's sudden flip-flop had instantly turned on whatever was lesbian in Lindsey-Smith; normally, it would've signaled schizophrenic behavior and sent her running. Lake was tall—five eleven—and buff. Even partially obscured by fog she stood out among the crime scene technicians and police personnel her bearing so feline-like. She had slanted almost black almond shaped-eyes that smoked. Her shoulder length hair swept severely back away from a high forehead that accented chiseled cheekbones giving her a look of intelligent rage that sent out the message don't mess with me. She wasn't pretty, but oh that ass. Seldom, had Lindsey-Smith ever seen reason to break her own rules, especially that one about never messing with dangerous women.

Over Lake's shoulder Lindsey-Smith noticed flashlights bouncing beams off the ground where suddenly a gust of wind snatched away the gloom exposing matted long dark hair lying like a wig near a decayed-once-upon-a-time white dress— ghastly against the Halloween night's melodramatic fog. Unable to pull her eyes away she squeezed them shut. A throaty voice, not hers, whispered, *the elements and critters had their way with Serena, too. A mutt gnawed on Serena's tibia, too. Took it home to its master who didn't have a clue it was human.* She pried open her eyes.

A dog barked in the woods.

"I can't do this."

"Good." Lindsey-Smith heard Boggs declare on the other side of the clearing to investigators.

Lake tugged on Lindsey-Smith's sleeve. "Are you okay?" She didn't wait for an answer. "Let's get you out of here."

"Hell, no!" Her jaws clenched and unclenched rippling muscles under the flawless complexion she inherited from her mother. She heard the barking quicken. Her heartbeat followed suit. "Is that the dog that found her...uh bone?"

"That's our Canine Unit."

"You don't have to say it twice. I need to get away from here. There's that song I'm supposed to be writin. The deadline's kickin my ass."

"Amazin. You can write a love song after what you've seen here." She pointed her flashlight in the direction of the corpse.

Fog came between them. "If I can't my career's screwed. I've got a once in a lifetime opportunity. Blow it and who knows... well I'm not gonna get negative."

"How much have you written?"

Lindsey-Smith held up a middle finger, "One line." She crooned: "*If I lose...if I lose you I've lost tomorrow. All my beginnings and all my todays.* Two lines now."

"Sounds like one of Luther Vandross' lost that love songs.

No offense; you're talkin bout losin love. I thought you said they wanted an *up* love song. You know with a happy endin?"

Lindsey-Smith shrugged. It didn't require a critique. She immediately regretted opening herself up. "It's bout the melody, right now."

Lake shrugged. "I'm tone deaf."

She wrinkled her nose. Great. She was dating a woman who couldn't hear. "Can I borrow your flashlight?"

"Give me a minute to get somebody to escort—"

Miffed, she cut her off. "I can find my own way. Just walk towards the lights." She nodded towards the smear of lights in the distance.

Lake handed over the flashlight. "Look, Lindsey. I know how hard this must be. I'm sorry you had to see it. Well, you know if you want to talk bout it...." She tucked away her soft side. "I'll call ahead. Let the canine units know you're comin. Guess this is the last time you'll go out with me, if you've got any sense."

"What if you don't catch him, Lake?"

A worried expression wrapped around Lake's face like a sarong. Her eyebrows knitted together. "We'll catch the mutha." She said all full of confidence.

Lindsey-Smith's temperature roiled. "Except most of the time you cops don't. You never caught my sister's killer."

The new information coupled with rage, threw Lake off. She quickly recovered as was her style. "Huh...your sister was murdered? Why didn't you say something instead of standin here holdin all of that in?"

Twenty years of rage, she couldn't pull it back. She didn't want to. "Statistically, I've got as much chance of catchin him as you do." She stalked off leaving the fog to blame for her vanishing act.

5

"Damn dog." Lindsey-Smith fussed at the barking dog as she trudged along. Although she couldn't see the dog she could see something: a black two-dimensional boxy human shape flashed through the rolling mist. Its two trapezoidal heads atop flat square shoulders jerked sideways as if to check out each other. As quickly as the shadow arrived it disappeared leaving her to wonder if an over heated mind conjured up the whole thing.

"Bitchin dog." She blamed and complained groping her way, summing up the day. "In mere hours I've gone from eatin sushi from Lake's gorgeous body to lookin upon a child's remains to talkin to a barkin dog in milky woods. Halloween. Why the hell not?"

She was grateful for one thing; in five hours Halloween would end forever.

A dog barked once, sharply. A clear warning. A tightening sensation crawled between her shoulder blades. Her visceral reaction to the barking dog was mild compared to her mother's reaction that required tranquilizers.

A morbid chill blew on the back of Lindsey-Smith's neck. She massaged the spot judging the warning. A deep-throated growl challenged her next step.

A police radio transmitted tiny firecracker explosions.

"Detective...I mean Lieutenant Lake called bout me." She shouted into the fog at shapes moving towards her. The dog responded. "You got a problem with that dog, officer?" The pissed dyke asked and was taken aback by an Icabod Crane silhouette.

"Down, Symbol! Down!" The dog ceased barking. "Didn't see you."

"Would that be you or the damn dog?"

Suddenly, German Shepard's teeth clicked centimeters from her throat. She jumped back unable to avoid the paw that raked a four-lane highway down her cheekbone. And she was twelve years old again, except her mother wasn't there to save her from the big bad doggy. Unbidden, the pink gun appeared in Lindsey-Smith's tremulous hand.

Icabod straddled the Shepard's back; his grip on the beast's collar—tenuous.

"Get away from him, officer!"

His eyes stuck to the bouncing gun. "Is it real?" The dog went berserk.

"I swear I'll shoot you both. Back off!" Suddenly the dog lay down and whined.

"What the…? I swear, this isn't supposed to happen. It's like weird. What's the matter, boy?"

Lindsey-Smith's head snapped in the direction in which the dark apparition appeared before the dog attacked. *Weird* had been the word that leaped to mind then. And now.

"Is that a real weapon?" Suspicion edged aside the officer's apologetic tone.

She caught his drift. "Look at my face." It burned lava hot. Blood trickled down her chin. "You are so sued. That dog did this to me. And your ass wants to talk about a gun. Who's gonna pay for my plastic surgery? You? The dog? He works for the city."

Icabod wrapped an arm around the cowering dog's neck. "He's an awesome dog. If you report her it's over for us. I'll pay. Anything. Please. Is that a real gun?"

With the sleeve of her black shirt Lindsey-Smith wiped blood from her face. Her mind slipped into reality. She couldn't use the police, not to mention Lake, looking at her gun. "If I didn't need a doctor like right now…." As her voice trailed she glared at the dog not trusting it to remain docile. "Forget we ever met." Until I sue you her litigious brain added.

"Nobody ever forgets meetin me. Particularly if they meet me on All Saints' Night. It's my profile."

She shook her head. It was time to make a get away and take care of her face. She scanned the fog for the two-headed shadow. "Trust me when I tell you there're other things people can't forget. It's not a choice—forgettin. It's how we choose to remember things we want to forget."

"How's that workin out for you?" He pointed to his prominent Adam's apple. "You can always tell when it's Halloween. I eat too much candy." He swallowed hard, bobbing his Adam's apple up and down, then turned sideways, and gave her his Icabod profile.

6

Twenty minutes after JP fled Possum Woods he nestled inside a parked panel van examining a four-ounce bottle containing his tonic. He put off using it.

His attention refocused on voices in his earphones that were attached to illegal listening equipment. From a quarter of a mile away he could hear reporters asking questions that only he could answer. In the comfort of his superiority he giggled as he turned down the volume on the police scanner to the level it had been when he heard dispatch rumble about the discovery of skeletal remains in Schiller Forest Preserve.

His first rule: keep your friends close—he had none of those—keep your enemies even closer; he had his share of those; he knew them but they didn't know him. The rule mandated that he spy on the police when they discovered his products.

To insure that he picked up minimal chatter and minimize his exposure he scouted every crime site for the perfect listening post. Recordings existed of every scene he visited. He studied them daily. But this enemy was new, a recently formed special task force of investigators just for lil' ol him.

Pulsating lights dyed the cotton candy world outside the van palace blue as they crept by with a siren screaming mercy.

"That's what I'm talkin bout." JP shouted triumphantly as he willed the squad car to keep on moving. In the vanity mirror he noticed a streak of blue light reflecting on his shaved head, uselessly, he swiped at it slapping himself on the head.

An excited buzz broke out among the reporters. Police officers commanded them to stay behind the yellow tape.

"Something's happening."

7

Lindsey-Smith slid behind the wheel of an ancient red Honda Accord that shouldn't have been on any public road. Yet, there it was by the grace of her shade tree mechanic. She turned the rearview mirror towards her and held her breath before checking out her cheek. Her breath caught in her windpipe. She blinked. It was worst than she thought.

From four vertical gouges seeped a thin ragged line of blood. Gone was the unblemished complexion she left home with hours earlier. That face—gone forever. Her world changed. "Go'damn dog!" She banged on the steering wheel. Four letter words she didn't know existed and some she made up exploded from her mouth. "This is money, baby. Your dog fucked my face up, Ic-cabod, you damn weirdo."

While her emotions messed with her composure she managed to speed dial on the cellular phone she clutched so tightly her knuckles ached. Her throat went dry.

After ten anguish filled minutes, she looked at her watch, it had been four minutes. She broke in on the one sided conversation and filled in the back-story in a one-line summary to her best friend Rita who only dated lesbian doctors. It was the next best thing to health insurance she had gleefully confided in Lindsey-Smith. A three-way conversation between three women, one a well-known plastic surgeon, followed. The bad day just didn't know when to quit. Thanks to the plastic surgeon she now added worrying about an infection to worrying about becoming scar face.

"Damn it. Damn it! My face." She would sue. The engine purred reminding her of Lake that night when a part-time friend pointed out the very hot detective as she strolled towards them, her predatory hips moving in a slow burning sizzle. As if transported she found herself standing chest to chest with Lake gazing into eyes that scorched her back. Lindsey-Smith asked, *are you wearin panties?* And watched Lake break then quickly recover with a purr. Then she asked, *can I have em?* And watched Lake choke on the words she was about to speak. Finally, she asked, *if they're wet then I know if I never get that pussy for one hot moment it was mine.* The detective arrested her. Maybe Lake could hunt down Mr. Crane and Symbol. "Which means I'm forced to see her again. God, I hate bein forced." She explained to her companion, Honda Annie.

The Accord answered; its gas gauge indicator sat on empty. "No way." She smacked the dashboard. "Get up there!" The gauge refused to move. Lights rushed at her like spirits emerging from the fog; unlike the gauge, she jumped. "Press? What the hell do you want?" Suddenly anger poured over her tongue and out of her mouth. Rolling the window down she yelled, "Damn ghouls, I don't know anything about the 7s Killer." Her Midwestern accent flattened vowels like Julia Childs' crepes. She revved the engine and threw the car into reverse. Ahead was an appointment to get her face back—maybe.

Reporters waving microphones jumped into the Accord's path and got for their stupidity horn blasts that, thanks to her mechanic, rivaled that of a Mack truck. "Ghouls!" The startled shitless expressions on reporters' make-up plastered faces and their scattering bodies would've been funny any other time in any other place.

Accord Annie roared out the parking lot.

JP's black van tailed.

Stiffness—an inner alert signal—crawled into Lindsey-Smith's neck. As she messaged it she checked in the rearview mirror and saw nothing but fog. "Fine!" She turned off the lights and rolled around a corner.

JP brought the van to a dead stop in the middle of the street. Its headlights were alien eyes searching for life. Nothing. He honked the horn in angry staccato out bursts.

Halfway down the block Lindsey-Smith heard sharp horn

blasts and surmised she had had an unwanted companion. "Ghouls!" She stomped on the accelerator and immediately realized the danger of that and braked. Her face burned. If she could give back today she'd happily go back to her stressed-out self who, until now, she had wished she could change.

The vintage Tag Hauer on her left wrist read seven o'clock. There was more than enough time to make her doctor's appointment. Yet misfiring nerves continued to accelerate the car.

The thought occurred to call a friend, run her mouth to distract herself until she arrived in Oak Park. Instead, she turned on the I-Pod affixed to the dashboard. Patrice Rustin's buttery voice flowed to her center calming the quivers in her stomach and settling the brain waves that frenetically bounced from visions of forever disfigured to yesterday's face to Lake's face.

"You can do this." She wanted to touch it but could imagine all the germs swarming on her hand entering her face...flesh eating staphylococcus. "Stop it."

She returned to the music. To tighten up her self-esteem she played one of her own songs: *I met a man the other day. Speak of the devil.* She switched off the music. A looming deadline demanded that she work on the newest song.

Rage disoriented JP, forced him to whip a u-turn, and forced him to recognize the seeds of fear taking root in his gut as he raged at the occupant of a red car long gone. "Who are you?" He yelled, pounding on the horn. Spent, he gathered his fragmented edges and willed himself to focus. He'd seen the task force in a news conference held to introduce them. So who was this lady that called him the 7s Killer? JP hated the sound of the name. "Cunt!"

Just the thought of the press running with that name pissed him off good. As he drove back to his listening post he caught the sound of humming coming from the package. "Hey, that's my song." He joined in: *Jesus loves the little children, all the children of the world. Red and yellow black and white—*

People said there were no red or yellow people. He knew

better. He always knew better. Pink and yellow were the only skin undertones no matter the race. Since forever make-up had been made based on that. Blacks, unlike whites, often called pink tones red. That knowledge worked his disguises. The humming stopped. JP's rage returned. "7s Killer!" He didn't blink until he drove by the crime scene.

Investigators and the coroner were in a lively discussion about him, or rather who they assumed him to be. The investigators, Chicago PD's best detectives, didn't know squat about him. Not one assumption touched him. As reassuring as that was his rage barely subsided.

His disrespect for the investigators grew from a molehill into a familiar mountain. The one thing they did know about him he summed up, "I'm not a monster. Ninety-eight percent conviction rate. Accommodations. Awards. That shit won't catch me." Unimpressed by Lake's arrest record, JP turned up the volume.

8

It was eleven o'clock when Lindsey-Smith checked the yellow and black Tag Hauer sports watch that she nicknamed the bee. Since time was relative she had named every watch she ever owned. The ridiculous reasoning made her smile on one side of her face. The other side, frozen into place by the plastic surgeon, didn't budge. And neither did the fog.

Taillights bleeding in front of her veered left. She followed maintaining one hundred feet between her and them. She heard the traffic—freeway. Rusty cold water pumped through her veins to her brains.

Brain freeze.

What a huge mistake: freeway and fog.

Too late, she rolled with cotton balls the size of Hummers. That morbid chill returned, flicked its serpent tongue from her nape down her spine to the crack in her butt. An environment like none she'd ever felt before spilled over her. The cotton thickened into a roux.

Taillights.

By the time she thought it the Accord rear-ended the wide butt of a white Volvo causing a chain reaction. Steam from her car's crumbled hood mingled with fog as she attempted to back up only to discover that she had clamped onto the Volvo's bumper. They moved where the pile dictated.

She snared the door handle. It fell into her hand. "Whyyy?" She released the seat belt, scrambled over the console into the passenger seat just as a window opened in the fog where a hearse driven by a headless old man swished by. Behind it ran a silver Rolls Royce steered by nothing more than a pair of porcelain white hands with long red nails, the left one Lindsey-

20

Smith noticed blinged with a fat diamond engagement ring, and behind the Rolls roared a sunshine yellow Porsche convertible driven by a head cut from gray poster board. From it sprang a grinning mouth full of chrome piranha teeth. The parade ended in the next one of her thousands of inadvertent blinks a day.

The parade had lasted less than a blink in time. Her guts coiled. She blinked several times in an attempt to conjure up the images. But they had long ago returned to the fog, or to her imagination. She must've dinged her head damn hard on the headrest when she crashed. She slowed her jets and ordered self under control. Death was guaranteed if she remained in the car, exiting with just feet of visibility was suicide. She weighted them and took her chances. She bailed.

Headlights bled through the gauze. Disoriented, it was impossible to tell how far she was from the right lane. If she could get there she could climb the embankment to the street. With that plan in mind she gave it up and scampered. A moment later, still disoriented, she stopped. Not until then did she fully connect to the sound of tires skidding, the sickening crunch sound that only crashing cars deliver, women and grown men crying out for help, and her own breathing. The sounds arrived muffled to her ear, yet she heard the sound of tires slapping against wet pavement.

Lindsey-Smith found her scrawny butt in headlights that raced her up the embankment. With a stolen glance over her shoulder her peripheral vision was horrified to tell her brain that their ass lost the race.

Before her brain processed death a white limousine t-boned the demon shoving it away from her. To the fanfare of blasting car horns, she climbed over the fence. "I can do without the horn section," came squealing off her scared lips.

Shook up she talked herself down. "I could've done without the woods, for sure. Now I'm gonna be stuck with the image of that baby's headless skeleton the rest of my life."

No more would she image Serena's body, as she was when she last saw her—alive and well. She would forever be that pathetic skeleton in the woods undiscovered.

Perhaps it was the reason she was sent into the woods, to get real.

9.

"Transportation challenged." Lindsey-Smith corrected, barking into her phone. "Of course. It *was* a tight ride." She rolled her eyes skyward. "Now get up off the couch and come get me, or I'll forget your fluffy kids this Christmas." It was a ploy that always worked him.

She took a few unsure steps in the fog. "Can't see the street signs. Don't go there. I'm not lost. Just don't know where I am. There's a difference you know, my some-timey friend."

Swish swish. Silky fabric rubbed together somewhere behind the layers of fog. A red streak lunged at her. Off balance, sidestepping, she dropped her cellular. Her eyes darted right. Left. Right. Left.

"Git him!" A tinny voice yelled.

A rush of red exploded out of the bloozy air at her, simultaneously, she fell back squeezing off several wild shots.

"Muthafucka shot me!" Tinny voice quivered.

A hard blow struck the back of the woman's head. Her knees dug into pavement. Pain swung the world away from her in dizzying fuzz to a place where she heard gunmetal clank against concrete.

"He shot me." Tinny voice squealed disbelievingly.

Voices ganged up on her. "Git the fuckin gun, dawg." "Ahm bleedin." "You git the gun?" "Fuck naw." "Caint see shit, yall."

Red Timberland boots kicked her ribcage. She kicked back with size eleven pointed toe cowboy boots brutalizing flesh and bone. A toxic voice stammered, "Sh…sh…shit! He broke my fuckin knee."

It dawned on Lindsey-Smith that the gangbangers had mistaken her for a man. Hands swarmed into her pockets. A rough hand grabbed her by the hair and snapped her head back. Soon they'd feel her breasts and it would be over. Suddenly the mysterious clanking sound made sense to her. And the cold hard object on which her butt sat had the unmistakable shape of a gun.

She shoved it in the closest face.

"Do it!" A sonorous voice took control. The owner of the voice leaned closer. A smile snatched his gold-laden mouth sideways. If he got any closer he would see that she was not a he.

Blood dripped into her right eye forcing her to blink. Goldteeth slapped the barrel away from his face. In a desperate effort, she managed to kick his feet from under him. On his feet quick as a whip snake, Goldteeth lunged at her. She stuffed the barrel in his crotch.

A finger tatted up with jailhouse ink pointed at the gun when he issued a directive to his minions, "Chill!" Eyeing her through mist he cooed around a mouth of gold, "Please, Ahm cool, dawg. Yall, give him back his shit."

A brown leather wallet landed in her lap followed by her precious bee. Behind her in the Milky Way she heard a round jacked into a chamber. She froze.

Every electron in her body seized.

Lungs stopped breathing.

Heart stopped pumping.

Brain stopped thinking about tomorrow.

Stopped thinking about writing love songs.

BANG

10

On the six corners of North Avenue, Damen Avenue, and Milwaukee Avenue in Wicker Park where gentrification altered affordable housing to unaffordable for those who gave it the artist colony image—more than a dusting of heroine, crack, serial rapists, and homelessness rattled Mister Roger's hood.

In response, its yuppie insurgents, raised in a culture of money trumps everything, eventually, chose old-fashioned American denial and became the victims they denied. The historic buildings fronting artsy streets gave off a twenty-four seven vibe that labeled itself with a big fat name *eclectic something for everyone* was too long and unpretentious like its name change from Bucktown to the more palatable Wicker Park.

True enough, people came. All types of people.

Traffic, normally congested, was non-existent. A parade of gray figures: a devil walking on his tippy-toes, a headless zombie, and a swan emerged and entered the fog walking west on North Avenue. Then along came Frankenstein's Bride strolling east.

Out of nowhere a warm liquid splattered her eyes. Wiping frantically with the back of her hand the bride whimpered. She opened her mouth to scream. Hot liquid rolled in. She swallowed. She screamed. Then couldn't. She couldn't see. On fire, her face melted in her hands.

"I'm invisible now, rich bitch?" A voice came and went in the murk.

11

Thump thump thump!

Disoriented, Lindsey-Smith laying face down in a gutter struggled to maintain consciousness if for no other reason than to figure out what the hell made the disturbing thumping noise.

Thump thump thump!

She tried to swallow but found her heart in her throat.

Thump thump thump!

The thumps played andante at first then shot to presto when her common sense got into the game shooting adrenaline through her DNA. Her eyesight went blurry. But she saw the clotting blood and splatter of brains, and bone fragments that peppered her black leather jacket. She took stock of herself. Couldn't be her brains. She was alive. Full-blown panic sat her upright too fast.

"Oww. Oww. Owww!" Breath-snatching pain stabbed her heart. "Oww. Owww! A heart attack? On top of everything else I'm havin a heart attack?" She cried incredulously. It took a minute before she realized the pain generated from her ribcage not her heart. "Oh yes. Oh yes." Better her ribs than her heart. She eased out of her favorite leather jacket careful not to make contact with the gore. "Ouch, damnit!"

Damp cold rushed over her. It chilled the marrow in her bones. Urgent hot blood trickled from her temple. She had to get on her feet. Find her phone. "My face?" Panicked, she touched her face and found the bandage still in place. But her fingers were sticky. "Blood." She vaguely remembered passing out. There would be another scar. "Just screw me!"

Lindsey-Smith gritted her teeth until she pulled herself

26

through the pain to her feet. Unsteady, her knees genuflected almost tossing her back in the gutter. As she steadied herself headlights riding high approached. They either belonged to a truck or a bus she decided. She pulled for the bus.

While she waited knots swelling on her battered head throbbed in sync with her pulse. Like a drum skin she was tight. Blood congealing on her swollen bottom lip felt like a Maraschino Cherry sticking out the corner of her mouth.

Her eyes were Kalamata Olives in a Bloody Mary. Fido's scratches were the least of her worries because cracked ribs demanded sharp attention with every breath. Her teeth clenched permanently.

A Chicago Transit Authority bus emerged from layers of white curtains. It stopped. The doors opened. The bus driver, a tiny woman, took one horrified look at the bloody disheveled addict about to step on her bus, closed the doors, and floored it.

"Aint mad at you, lady." Lindsey-Smith held her head. That said it all. No sane person was gonna pick her up the way she looked." She looked worst than she imagined.

A soft cushy object brushed against her left shoulder.

"You grabbed my titty." A low rough female voice charged.

"You couldn't pay me to do that."

The woman put her hands on her hips and swung her weave over a shoulder before taking the hoochie stance. "Wha'cha mean, be'atch?" The woman asked offended. Her body poised to pounce, and then backed off. She jammed a forefinger at Lindsey-Smith's head. "What dat?" She snapped.

"What?" She asked confused at the woman's sudden shift.

Still pointing the woman insisted, "In yo hair, stupid be'atch."

The battered one shook her head flinging bits of brain and bone in the direction of the woman. A barber's razor materialized between the woman's fingers as she slashed a *z* in the air and ran at one pissed dyke.

"Git the fuck up off me, be'atch." The woman screamed coming at Lindsey-Smith.

That scene from the movie *Indiana Jones* where he confronts a man swinging a sword flashed in front of her. Pinky appeared in her hand. The sweet sound of feet slapping against pavement ran away from her. "Fuckin ghetto rat! I'm the wrong dyke to fuck with tonight. What's up world? Why're you doin this to me?"

The effort shocked her ribcage injury into a bloody howl. Down the street she lurched hugging herself, feeling her way, groping buildings. She cursed every step. "Muthafuckas. You want a crazy dyke tonight, eat my shit and die." She cocked the gun. "Kiss my ass. I've been fucked for the last go'damn time. I got crazy for your ass." She fired the gun skyward. Tears rolled.

Ahead, she caught a glimpse of a red light flickering on an *open* sign before fog covered it, but then she couldn't trust her blurry eyesight. And to prove it a rumble broke out inside her skull between her brain and eyes. They didn't agree and argued like two adolescent siblings neither willing to give in without parental intervention. She sided with the sibling that insisted the sign was a hallucination.

Futilely she swiped blood from her leaky forehead with a shirtsleeve, without her cell phone she felt totally disconnected and in deep shit. Hopes of finding a business open on the Westside at this time of night boiled down to finding a liquor store or a tavern. On the Westside, they were all scary last time she noticed which was never. Still what choice did she have? She had to call a ride. One wasn't likely to materialize.

The apparition of the odd-shaped two-headed entity, it had gone from two-dimensional to three-dimensional, more a black smudge now, than a shadow, floated towards her. If hobbling counted as hurrying, she ran to confront it.

"Asshole, if I can shoot you you're real to me." She aimed pinky. "I killed a one-headed skank tonight. Two-headed mofos don't stand a chance." She squeezed the trigger. The smudge vanished into the fog. Before it did it looked long and hard at her. She felt it sit on her face.

With the last drop of will she possessed, she dragged her two-ton body, all one hundred and ten pounds of it, down the street. It was getting difficult to walk. Each step threatened to topple her. The red light flickered on the *open* sign.

"Yes! You're not a hallucination." A breeze blew across the back of her neck. She ignored the alarm and headed for the beacon. She had planned to call the police but changed her mind. No black person in their right mind would make that call she reasoned.

With that she lumbered down dark rickety steps.

12

Lindsey-Smith dropped in. She rolled her sore eyeballs around a short and narrow tavern. *Circa* 1940, she decided. Fermented in cheap whiskey and stale smoke, all in all, it was a dingy dim geezer hangout.

Not one of them looked in her direction. At the end of the bar only one barstool stood vacant. She willed her body to it. Her butt swiveled onto the well-worn stool as she reassessed the hole-in-the-wall, checking a window up front the size and shape of a ship's portal. It was cloaked in fog. She shook her head. What an idiot. Did she expect to see the ocean?

Swooning she griped the bar. Over the decades the dark stained wood had been assaulted with cigarette burns, carved messages, and overlapping whiskey rings. Behind it, a streaked mirror, its reflection tortured by patches of missing silver nitrate, presented the dyke with the face of a leper. She was missing the tip of her nose and an eye. Otherwise, she looked fine. Sure she did.

"Bartender, a diet cola and a phone, please." The bartender glanced disinterestedly at her making no effort to move. "You help me out here?" She noticed that the cherry on her lip made her sound as if she lisped. The right side of her face lost the Botox effect. Yet nothing hurt. Her whole body was pain free. But she remained elegant. "Fucker." She muttered. "Ten dollars, bartender, for one local call." She lisped patronizingly.

The coke arrived without fizzle in a rocks glass sans ice.

"Got no ice." The bartender muttered slamming down the glass before her.

She examined the dark liquid. "What the hell's that?" She spluttered.

"Cola. Regular." The bartender said secretly through a toothless-smiling mouth.

She scanned the geezers for reactions. It seemed to her that they drank determinedly as if they were duty bound. The arm action, glass to mouth seemed mechanical. She'd seen that before. Unable to place it, she pushed the drink aside, "How bout that phone?"

The bartender shrugged. "In fifty years I never seen need to get one." He scuttled away—kind of on the quick side for an old man, she observed.

"It's against the law not to have a phone in a public business." She preached to the retreating backside.

"You sho make a valid point." Agreed a mole-like man; so old she noted that his skin was like black parchment. The man, who sported a dusty black cape, glanced to his left at her. He smelled like a rodent, too, though she had never smelled one. She tried not to inhale in his direction.

"Does this face look like it wants to have a conversation?"

"Looks to me like it done had one serious conversation."

"Bartender, this hole got an address?"

The old man cleared his throat. "You don't know where you at. Sad. You got a funky attitude for somebody who's lost." He shook his rodent head in disbelief.

The desire to choke the dusty old man came on her suddenly. She shook it off, but the certainty remained that something bad had touched the fog. Her intellect popped her on the head. What the hell kind of fog is that? It wasn't predicted.

"It's the devil's work, the ol folks usta say."

She would've laughed if she didn't fear it might hurt. "Old folks? Check it out. You're old folks. In case you didn't remember."

"Check it out. The better thought would've been ol man how you know what Ah was thinkin?"

"Fuck you."

"You love the taste of pussy. We got that in common."

Lindsey-Smith's conversation dried up like a drop of water on the Mohave Desert at high noon. The old man casually examined his sallow fingernails. His beady rodent eyes shifted to the wall clock above the bar's mirror.

"It's eleven-fitty." He announced solemnly.

"Don't talk to me!" She pronounced each word with exaggerated emphasis.

"Ten minutes lef fo Halloween runs out on us. *Us* would be me and you."

With that her head became a spinning top. Got to get away from here. The portal delivered the final say-so: *you're going nowhere, girlfriend.*

The old man clicked his fingernails together like castanets. It creped her out. "Please, don't do that. Please." The old man's tarry eyes went red; his fuzzy white tongue uncurled, licked away a white viscous fluid from his chin. No lesbian should have to see a tongue like that. Immediately, she set out to ban it from her memory.

"You aint goin no place. At least you got that much right. Listen to me if you wanna live. When midnight come round me and yo fool ass gonna be shit outta luck. We'll be Miss CINNN-dee-rella, a raggely ass be'atch standin behind a big ass orange punkin with fo mice darin us to touch it." A grin crept onto the old man's desiccated lips. She ignored him.

Delivered of the awkwardness of being caught staring, he preyed on Lindsey-Smith's profile trying to read a woman adapt at not being read. If he read her wrong he'd become a lowly minion. He was old as dust because he read people right. Just thinking about the reward for her soul pumped spasms into the shrunken cock that twitched against ancient thighs. He felt all eighteen inches swell to its three-inch diameter. Bubbles came out and dripped down a decrepit thigh. Part of his pay would be getting outfitted with a pair of sixteen-year-old legs for ten hours. He drank Viagra. This bitch wasn't going to fuck up his eternity, get him screwed inside out into a minion. He could smell that aged cherry perched next to him. He s'pected he'd be stickin his toothpick in that.

Under his cape the ancient stroked his stiff motivation as if he were back in the day when he showed off a stolen new 1932

Ford Roadster. Chests stuck out, the church ladies just couldn't stay out of the shiny car's rumble seat come Sunday walking in their high heel shoes with barking feet. That virgin pussy so sensitive, he sucked his tongue, '... *this aint the real deal sex, baby. Naw. It's somethin special Ah made up just fo the ladies to keep them cherries from goin sour on the vine.' With the tip of his thumb he rubbed her aroused nipple to erection. 'Taint nothin but a juicy butterfly kiss relievin you of yo hoochie juice. You know you got too much up in there to keep that cherry ripe. One juicy kiss.' He slid a hand between her thighs and rubbed the silky panties until they turned wet. Inside, he stroked the hair above her virgina until cream covered the follicles. She yelped, 'Opps.' When she came unexpectedly. He stuck a finger in the cream. 'That's what Ahm talkin bout.' He slurped his fingers thanking her profusely. 'That's all it is, suga. Can Ah do this to you?' He ran his six-inch tongue between her fingers as he lifted her hips. Once he had that butt turned up he ran his tongue through the cream. Her snapping abyss snared his plunging swirling tongue squeezing it against walls it tickled the softening cherry. Teased it with quick flickers befitting a feather. Screaming 'Lordy help me' as her back arched, she seized. When she dropped she dragged his head to her clit. 'Butterfly me, daddy.' He sucked and smacked his lips. He slapped the clit repeatedly with his tongue, each time dragging his long long long velvet tongue across the swollen virginity. 'Eat that coochie up', she begged. 'Harder. Daddy, do it hard. Yes, like that. Faster. Like you want them cherrrrrries. Daddyyyyyyyy!' He wrapped the hard clit in his tongue and vibrated it. Then popped it out of his mouth. It was red. Angry. So he sucked it hard. 'Harder. Harder.' She banged the greedy thing raw. Hoarse, she begged him 'gemme some dick. Hurry up, Lord have mercy, daddy. Make that bitch bleed. They yo cherries.' He swore he'd stop and he did. He liked to say he stopped lickin and started stickin. First he showed her his knob. Big as her wee little fist. She pleaded with him not to stick it in her. 'Let me see yo pussy grab ahold of this here.' He drilled all eighteen inches inside the plushest pussy he ever fucked. Some had long pussy some had short pussy; none had long enough pussy. He ripped himself a path through the cherry field and beyond. He pulled his bloody dick out so he could ram it in real good. When he did, low and behold he plucked another cherry. He got harder than he ever been. Two hours later, unfortunately for him, he lingered too long on some tasty tappin and caught a nappy head full of lead. He smacked his dried lips together. There was one good thing that came of it. He died having the best orgasm he ever had. He heard in the morgue that he shot off three ounces into both vaginas. He heard he fucked a didelphic uterus—two vaginas, two cervices, two uteruses, two cherries and they fucked him to death. That thirty-year-old double virgin pussy had tasted like Merlot even though he never tasted the wine.* Licking his lips he sized up Lindsey-Smith. He could damn near taste her red wine.

The time was eleven fifty-six when he looked at the clock again. He sucked his tongue. "Ssss. Ah work one day a year. You know, like San-tee Clauze." He sniffed. "You smell like fine wine."

"Come down my chimney and I'll blow your dusty butt away. Don't talk to me."

"Shit. Been talkin to yo ass all night. Eleven fitty-six, baby girl. And countin. Fitty- two seconds fitty-three seconds. In ma business ev'ry second counts, you dig?"

Chinese gongs went off in Lindsey-Smith's head. "You mean at your age every second counts." She saw the blue tail of a serpent slither up his narrow nostril. Her nose wrinkled. Oh boy, she was seeing things.

"Ah know what the fuck Ah mean. You know, you got death's putrefied scent all over you. Hangin with ghouls gits you skunky like that."

"Could you just shut up?" She blamed the damn fog.

"Ah figured you fo someone who believes in ghouls when you fell up in here."

She nodded. He aint right. Everything about the place was off. Damn, the whole night was off. Rapidly she summed up her sorry position: She was stuck here. Pain free. Had been since she sat down, which should've make her cry like a baby with gratitude. So why was it worrying her? "Cause you know it aint right." She muttered under her breath.

"You sittin there breathin cause you survived the gauntlet." He pretended to shiver as he wrapped his cape tightly around him. He pouted, "Porcelain weddin hands. Cardboard head with the shiniest chrome piranha grill you ever wanna see—"

She cut him off. "Who are you?"

"Ahm the go'damn man that's here to grant you a Halloween wish."

"Oh, shut up!" She covered her ears and noticed that it didn't hurt to lift her arms. Wow!

"Ah do that we both die to-night." He felt his foot slipping on the rim. "You believe in ghouls. That's the only pre-requisite. If you fail to achieve yo wish you die. Ah die. Ah don't die well."

A harsh laugh rattled out of her chest. "I know how this works. I read that fairy tale. A man makes three wishes. Instead of endin up with a bigger dick, he ends up a go'damn whale in some ocean with a whale of a dick. Prove otherwise."

"This aint no fairytale. One wish, muthafucka. Ah said *one wish.*" He had one minute and thirty-eight seconds left in this life. "Aint got time fo yo attitude. Allow me to adjust it."

1-3

Lindsey-Smith stood stock-still on a dirt road in the woods. She freaked then tried to run. Paralyzed, wild-eyed, she followed the shaft of light sent out by the crescent moon to a sign that read: POSSUM WOODS FOREST PRESERVE.

At least her eyes moved. That slowed her freak-out and allowed her to gather her senses.

The world in which she found herself appeared concave, like reflections in carnival mirrors, though in color it was at once a cold and bleak world. Faded.

Her brain questioned her whereabouts. It wanted to know what was happening to her.

A few feet in front of her she saw a pale red Volkswagen that continued to pale as she stared at it. White cracks radiated from a hole in the driver's side of the windshield. Behind the wheel slumped a ghostly white young man with Afro-centric features and a hole between his eyes beneath which glistened a red teardrop. Her eyes clung to the teardrop.

Abruptly released from the transfixion she jerked around, grabbed the old man by his collar, and yelled in his face, "What the hell was that?" His cape dropped open releasing funk that knocked her back. Three legless thighs looked up at her. Little pointy mustard teeth wedged in red gums grinned at her.

He closed his cape. "That's yo proof. What's yo wish? You got sixty-eight seconds to git rid of yo ghoul with this caveat. You don't kill it, nobody will."

Badly shook, head spinning, nothing made sense except the ghoul. How did he know? Just touching on the thought aggravated the rage already out of the barn. The stewed taste of pent up revenge, blood from biting her tongue during the transfixion in Possum Woods, fueled her. Serena's killer is long gone. If she couldn't get him she would get the one she could.

"What the hell. You want a dark wish just perfect for Halloween? You know what I wish? I wish I could get in the 7s Killer's head just long enough to catch a clue to kill his ass and cut off—"

She was on her hands and knees under a tree, inside a monster's body. Inside its head watching currents flow snag misfire; no landscape there resembled a conscience. She viewed the world through eyes that lowered to glare into pools of terror spilling from the doe eyes of a girl. She him they straddled the child. Disbelieving she screamed *NOOOO* in her head. Repulsion cramped her guts. Her brain pleaded. She changed her mind. She wanted out. She wanted to go back to life before Lake got that terrible call about a body in the woods.

Her eyelids seemed to be glued open to the concave world, its white textures reminiscent of photographs that she vaguely recalled seeing in a photography book of Arlington Cemetery. A photographer had used a special camera to capture light that the human eye couldn't see. It was the light between two worlds.

Her fingers tingled.

My hands...his hands not mine...his hands around the girl's tiny neck. A soft mewling sound came from the child and tore Lindsey-Smith's heart from its cage. Her his brain chanted, *It's mine...it...Cindy.* The girl's terror-struck eyes reached inside the woman and singed her soul. She felt the girl's neck snap in her...no...in the monster's hands. She felt her his...*HIS* sexual surge. She felt Cindy's last breath brush against her wounded cheek.

Lindsey-Smith Cutter changed forever.

Then she was back on the barstool. Icy sweat bled from every pore. She jumped off the stool. Pain returned with a vengeance when she saw that the old man's stool was empty. She checked the clock. It was five seconds after midnight. Halloween had mercifully ended.

"Bartender, where'd the legless ol bastard go?"

He shrugged his sloped shoulders, "Legless? Him? You alive. Count yourself lucky he left."

"Left? How?"

"The way he came."

"Annnd what way would that be?" She fumed.

"Walkin."

"He didn't have legs, fool."

"It remains to be seen who's the fool up in here."

"You know don't you?" She asked accusingly. "Did the 7s Killer really murder a little girl?" The geezers sneered in response. Just beyond them fog vanished from the portal. Lindsey-Smith hobbled out of the joint faster than her injuries liked.

XXXX

10:02 pm. Halloween. Three thousand miles from Chicago horizontal rain from a mean black California sky slashed traffic that corkscrewed up and down the Pacific Coast Highway (PCH), home to the highest peak in America, outside of Alaska. Out of respect, in a dark Kia SUV, gay partygoers, Bush Junior and Senior, and Freddy Krueger, raised lollipop drinks in a toast. A road sign warned: WATCH FOR FALLING ROCKS.

On one side of the treacherous highway the Sierra Nevada Mountain range loomed. Its jagged saw teeth dominated the air space. Hundreds of feet below the highway, the Pacific Ocean crashed fifty-foot waves against the mountain's craggy feet. Ironically, those who were forced to swerve to miss falling rocks risked death by veering off the mountain.

A vintage orange Corvette caring nothing about horizontal rain and corkscrew turns, shot around the Kia and rode up on a black Escalade's big Bertha-butt. The Corvette braked and spun out then fishtailed to a stop. Raindrops separated it from a grill to grinning grill head-on collision with a black Mercedes.

Behind the Mercedes' steering wheel Dracula, empty sockets where eyes should've been, glared at the Corvette's driver who couldn't possibly know why he chased her, nor that driving-while-orange was deadly on Halloween that year, unanimously voted so by all in attendance at the First Annual

Devil's Associates Convention, scheduled hence forth on every Halloween through eternity.

To be chosen as *it* was the highest honor. Only the bravest souls became *it*.

Over the initial shock of surviving, the fiberglass body reversed then scampered away leaving an orange streak in panes of black diamond rain. She raced as fast as the tires would take her in spite of climbing in the rain.

Dracula's bald companion twisted her swan neck into a pretzel and dove on his dead dick. The Mercedes surged. "How's it feel to be dead?" She slurped.

He grabbed swan neck, jerked her head up, "Not as bad as I thought it would feel." He laughed. With the gas petal to the floor the Mercedes hydroplaned and took off around the mountain and over lesser vehicles. "Where she at?" He touched down.

14

"Condemnment two: 'Damned if I do, damned if I don't.'"
Satan flashed a toothy smile at his human mentor.

The man groveled, "For a place at your side I'm bringin your fav conquest to your Feast of Souls Table. I handed out murder propositions to the courageous few that damn them if they accept and damns them if they don't."

Satan's eyes bled.

Droplets fell away to earth.

15

When Satan bled the sky cleared. It was twelve forty-five according to the bee, which Lindsey-Smith felt lucky to get back from the gangbangers. Lake accelerated the GTV8 yellow Mustang convertible East onto the Eisenhower Expressway under stars flung against a cobalt blue sky.

Already, the city, survivor of weather events, had relegated the fog to water cooler status if the call-in radio show was to be believed. To Lindsey-Smith the fog had been alive. Its clammy presence still clung to her skin.

She cursed her noisy head for pressing the truth. If she was nappy hair she'd be straight. A girl named Cindy that's who was under her skin. What if she really existed...and the 7s Killer murdered her? Hell, how can that be? She had considered this over and over again while she waited for Lake to pick her up. Now her sanity was well—her insanity. If she continued down that path she could see herself strolling Uptown with plastic bags on her feet and a cup in her hand talking to herself. Still, she couldn't trust her brain.

"I'm talkin to you. Come back to earth. You know, I get why you don't want to involve the police. Look. You called me, remember? If you didn't want the police involved you should've called your other woman." Lake steered around a car doing less than eighty. "Get in the slow lane, be'atch." She cut a look at Lindsey-Smith. "I know an ass beatin when I see one."

"You really should see the other guy."

"Describe him and I'll see if I can make that happen, you know." Lindsey-Smith caught Lake's rolling eyes.

"I don't trust you with my sanity since you think it's

41

affected." She squinted through double vision at the Garfield Park Conservatory exit sign as they swished pass it.

That was nearly a night of exquisite pleasures. Chihuly glass sculptors flowering throughout exotic gardens. Jazz music. Jazzier woman. Tender hips in motion bumping side-to-side rubbing friction on all those licious clits. She licked the sore cherry growing on her bottom lip. The gardens' oppressive humidity had eventually deflowered the breath in her chest and left her panting for the wrong reason—pneumonia. A forever memory. Thank God, her long term memory functioned. "Do you believe in the supernatural?"

"I believe what I see."

"Me too." She thought about that. "I saw a girl murdered by the 7s Killer."

Lake's head snapped to her right. The car swerved. She brought it back into its lane. Her focus hardened. "Here's what I think. You've got a concussion. Your brain is doin a number on you. After seein that poor baby...what was left of her...lyin in the woods like that. You need to see a doctor, honey. You're hallucinatin. Big time."

"Do you know where Possum Woods is from here?"

"Why do you care?"

She didn't have the energy nor was she inclined to go through an explanation. What explanation? The knot on her temple beat the band. She needed to know if there was a dead man in a Bug to believe the impossible—that she witnessed a girl's murder. If she told Lake she might run them off the road. Lake's hand gently caressed her woman's thigh.

"Sore." She lied. Lake's hand slid away. Her reasonable questions had made Lindsey-Smith uncomfortable. "So where is Possum Woods?"

"Where's this goin? You do remember that you don't have a car...anymore."

Actually, she had forgotten. "What happened to my car?"

"You said you were in a pileup."

They passed The United Center. She blinked at her best sport memory, His Highness walking on air, his tongue hanging out, his cinnamon eyes flaming, he slammed the ball with such force awed grown men around her flinched. Another long-term memory intact. In the distance the Sears Tower loomed. She wondered if she could see the lights in three states from the observatory deck now that the fog had lifted.

"Right. Right." She agreed with herself. "I need a car." Her thoughts gathered themselves long enough to decide she couldn't afford to rent a car. "Come with me." Lake was right; Lindsey-Smith gave her that. Something was getting in the way of her memory. "Come with me anyway."

"Look. I'm tryin to get in a few hours of sleep here. By daybreak I'm due back at last night's crime site. Not that I'm ever up for chasin a hallucination."

"There's a dead man in Possum Woods. I need to find him. He's my proof."

"Aw crap, Lindsey. I thought you said you saw the 7s... damn it...the serial murder a girl?" She shot a distressed look at the dizzy woman.

"Cindy. He called her Cindy before he broke her neck." The Mustang slowed.

"We've kept the way the girls died from the public." Lake, her voice solemn and shaky croaked, "You...uh he called her Cindy?"

16

The beam bobbed up and down in the pitch-dark forest as Lake picked her way through the woods with Lindsey-Smith close behind nervously chatting away, "At least we can see. It's like the fog never existed. The ground's not even particularly wet. I'm tellin you, it's real odd, Lake." The path narrowed then disappeared beneath undergrowth. It was the third one to do so in the fifteen minutes since they struck out into Possum Woods.

"No, *this* is odd. I can't believe I'm out here in the... I can't say it it's so stupid." She held a tree limb away from Lindsey-Smith's face. "Watch it."

"It's not stupid. You're here cause I know that the killer didn't rape her and that he broke her neck. I shouldn't know that stuff. That's why you're here. You need proof just like I need proof." To ensure footing she dug her foot into the undergrowth. Every step, every movement, and every breath's bullish pain fought against seeing it through. Lake plunged ahead. "Reckless." She complained through gritting teeth pushing on for Cindy's sake, if she existed. "Wait." She barely got it out.

"You said this is what you want to do, Lindsey." Exasperated, Lake turned the flashlight on her, and then disappeared in the black forest behind the beam.

Lindsey-Smith looked into the floating light. Her wind trapped behind cracked ribs, she leaned against a tree. After a moment the words rushed out stumbling over each other as she described her journey to that concave universe that made up the wishscape. When she finished, she stole a breath and then a glance in Lake's direction. "There are only two things I ever wanted to do in my life...to write songs, and to revenge my sister's death." She dared to take a breath, damming pain behind clenched teeth she persisted, "About the only thing I can realistically hope for is to find her body and bring it home where she belongs with me and mom and dad. That's all I ever wanted. Hell, I don't want to be here. I don't want any of it." She shivered flashing on why she left her jacket on the street.

"You made your point. And here's mine, sweetie. I'll never talk to you again if we don't find a body."

"Fine. I'll be too embarrassed anyway." Already halfway to the vehicle, weapon in hand, Lake cautiously approached the red Volkswagen sweeping the area with her flashlight beam.

"God, I hate this. Hate it!"

"Aint technology wonderful? If base map software of Chicagoland woods didn't exist no way would we have found this road. And all the proof I need." She spied the bloody teardrop between the dead man's eyes.

Lake, wearing gloves examined the man's wallet. "Justin Banks. Accordin to his license he's twenty-two."

"It's true then. Cindy's out there." All the air escaped from her world. Her breathe caught.

Lake reared up in her grill yelling, "What have you done?"

She stood her ground refusing to flinch and catch pain for it then swallowed a sour taste. "Me? Come on, Lake. Tell me you know better than that."

"Thing is I don't know you. So I definitely don't know better than that."

"Oh really. You trusted me with the most precious thing you have to give." She pressed her hips into Lake's hips and pinned them against the Volkswagen's bumper.

Lake escaped. "The car's evidence, Lindsey. We didn't hook up."

"Almost. You got that call. Your intuition was it wrong?" Lake's heels dug into the dirt road. "You have two choices, Lieutenant Lake. Arrest me. Or, my personal favorite, we find Cindy. If I have to I'll do it by myself. I'll bring down the bastard by myself, too." She kicked dirt up. Her bottom lip already stuck out, she stuck it out even more.

"I can't leave here till I call this in." Lake said tightly.

"How long will that take?"

"To process the scene...the rest of the night."

"Cindy can't wait. You don't want her to wait, Lake. Think about it. She's gettin cold." Lake's BlackBerry chirped. Lindsey-Smith covered it with a hand.

"What do you want from me? I can't leave here before—" The phone wouldn't give up. "Lieutenant Lake!" She listened to the caller never permitting her eyes to stray from Lindsey-Smith who could see her mind weighing options. After a moment Lake's eyebrows pulled into a straight line, frowning she disconnected. "That was the head of the canine unit. Says he didn't have any men on duty last night. That his crew was all women. And he hasn't got a dog named Symbol."

"He's tryin to get out of bein sued."

"That's not the brotha's style." Lindsey-Smith had stopped listening.

"Barefeet. She's runnin barefooted through the forest. I know Cindy's T.O.D."

"What?"

"But I don't know where her body is." Panic pushed her voice up an octave. "I don't know where she is. Didn't see a park sign...I don't think."

"Where did you get the T.O.D?"

"From CSI. Time of death."

"Gemme a break with the TV." Lake glared. "Are you purposely bein obtuse? How on earth could you possibly know the T.O.D? That's what I'm askin. How?"

"You sure we're on earth?" She didn't have the energy to make up a story. "One minute I remember bits and pieces of the wishscape and the next minute I remember squat."

"Wishscape? It's got a name now?" She said putting down the notion.

"Nature abhors a vacuum. That's why every little thing has a name. Can't keep callin it whatever happened to me. Why not wishscape?" Excitement switched on. She saw a flicker she could use. "When he sna...." She couldn't use such a crude word. "I didn't know, Lake. I didn't know he was gonna do that to her. When he did, when he broke that baby's neck I tried to look away. I looked down. A watch. I saw just a wee glimpse of a watch with a crown on the face."

"Rolex."

"All day."

"Shit! The perp's got money. He can afford to be clever. But then, we suspected that cause of the way he throws money at the skanks. Too bad it took so long to confirm it. Then and again, I can't tell anybody it's confirmed, can I?" Lake snapped photographs of the footprints in front of the car. "Got two sets of tracks. Both about size nine. The shooter stood right here. "Awfully fuckin convenient you seein the time on his watch, you know." She stopped. "So what time was it?"

"Eleven fifty-nine. Yeah. Eleven fifty-nine. So what? By the time you find her it'll be academic." Her tone sagged. Overwhelmed she gave up. "Maybe hypnosis can help me remember stuff. Like the stuff I don't even know I know."

Lake continued snapping pictures. "You say you saw his watch. I believe you did. But, baby, that other shit? I don't know. That's freaky. That said I know you didn't bring me out here to give up. Findin this girl so soon after bein murdered increases our chances of findin evidence. Right now we got zip. Not even an eyelash. So tell me, which arm did he wear the Rolex on?" Lindsey-Smith touched her right wrist. "A lefty. You sure?"

"He had on latex gloves. Wonder why he wore two watches?" Confusion wrinkled her nose as she looked beyond the trees into that light that no human eye could see. "What kind of watch is *that*?"

17

It wasn't a time machine Lindsey-Smith had observed on the killer's left wrist. It was a GPS with coordinates on a wristband. The two women found themselves in yet another woods. The third woods visited in one night and Lindsey-Smith had her feel of outdoorsy pursuits for life. She couldn't stop scratching though knowing nothing crawled in autumn, except human slime. It was one fifty-seven in the morning when they arrived in the clearing in Schultz Forest Preserve.

Under a thin ray of moonlight black-spotted yellow-to-red ladybug carcasses sprawled like embroidery on the hem of the new white dress that adorned Cindy's corpse, which lay beneath a towering Christmas tree.

"She looks different." A child-like voice escaped from Cindy's witness as she scanned the girl's long black hair and the head turned too far right. "I'm sorry." She remembered the girl's mewling, the fear so palpable Lindsey-Smith felt it in her bone marrow. She'd been so caught up in comparing the real thing to the wishscape that she forgot about Lake until she heard her curse. "What're you doin?"

"Sendin pictures back to headquarters. Looks like he posed her. The right hand's reachin out. She's lookin at it. Maybe not." She cocked her head sideways and snapped another picture. "If he's posin them it could mean he's recreatin the seminal event. Or not." She clicked several pictures of the child's face then called it in.

Although the girl looked familiar it was her eyes that Lindsey-Smith knew her by, beyond that things were fuzzy and fragmented. Blessed with a better-than-average memory she knew a problem when it bit her hard. No longer could she rely on her best asset, her brain. Lake's mouth was still moving she noticed.

"I just sent photos of the vic. Put out an Amber Alert, West. Don't mention that she's deceased. They won't put out the alert if you do. It's just for livin vics." She disconnected and made three calls, the last one to the Forest Preserve PD. Finally, Lake addressed Lindsey-Smith, "Hell! Baby girl, don't tell anybody that story you spun for me. Today we lie. I hate me cause I know better." Lake chided herself. "You're the writer. Make up a story I can believe."

"That's your story to write. Don't even take me there. You're the cop."

Lake punched some keys on her BlackBerry. "That call you made for a ride lasted one minute and twenty seconds. Good. Keeps the lie shorter than the hair on my snatch."

"I wouldn't know, remember? We were interrupted and here we are."

"That cell, you bought it in a liquor store right?" She nodded wondering where Lake was going. "Good. Give it to me." Lake broke the cell into three pieces.

"Hey!" She protested too late.

Lake passed the pieces to her. "Toss em. Throwaways are untraceable. But my system will show your call. That call you made is the time it took for the serial or some scared witness to leave a tip on where to find the body. God help me. I'm gonna lose my job and go to hell. And you, please, don't talk."

"So why am I here, again? Chief Boggs will want to know."

"Hey, I have a life." To Lindsey-Smith Lake didn't sound so sure. Approaching sirens sounded in the distance. "That's the Forest Preserve PD. They're closer. Show time."

This time the woman who wished upon a star Halloween night sensed the shadow before she saw it. Its odd familiarity left an oily smudge on her singed soul. Both heads nodded then vanished. She bit down on a mouthful of burnt charcoal and tasted the crumbling bits. She washed it down with the taste of blood from her tongue.

18

At two in the morning when JP crawled into bed he heard cars being sent by dispatch to Schultz Forest Preserve. He kicked off the gray down comforter that swaddled his body. "Another one?" He shouted wondering what the odds were that two of his products would be discovered within hours of each other. The odds were so piss poor he knew something else had to be at play. His life went on red alert. People would die.

"Who found you?" He muttered pulling on a black hoodie. "Maybe it's a *what*. Another dog?" He shook his shaved head. "Naw, there go those odds again."

It came out of hibernation, the kind bears take when they're not quite sleep. That gnarly black thing set free so long ago during his enslaved childhood triggered an onslaught of profanity that cued images he couldn't stop: Svengoolian film featuring brown black bodies packed like vegetables suffocating souls abandoned in the Mojave Desert locked in truck Poppy and Black Mary starring baby Jesus.

Five newly drained sixteen-ounce bottles of water lay piled in the stainless steel kitchen sink where JP invariably came to after blacking out on a trip to the desert of his past. He gulped down the last sixteen-ounce bottle of mountain water, and then flipped it in the sink. Ninety-six ounces of water wobbled in his distended stomach with every movement he made towards the garage.

The traffic light on the corner down from JP's house changed to green. Action!

He followed the color back to a twelve-year old boy in a white Raggedy Ann dress; shoeless he creeps past squealing girls frolicking in a dolphin-shaped pool. They taunt the boy who ducks behind a planter where the cold toothy shadow of the Sierra Nevada's cut across his emaciated back returning him to the present.

As he motored past US Cellular Field lights hailing the World Champion White Sox turned night into day. Action.

Chlorine scented pool water drips from Jesus' seven-year-old mistress Suzy and friends. They corral him. Yank his ding-dong until their human doll drops a festive lollipop crafted in his image. *It's mine you can't have it* growls the gnarly thing that cuts loose and bites Suzy's face. It flees.

The Dan Ryan Freeway going north bottlenecked. JP slammed on the brakes and skidded into action.

Jesus runs pell-mell through forest-covered mountainside in bare feet. Suzy gains. He looks over shoulder, stumbles, learns never look back when his eyes fall on a red plaid picnic blanket wicker basket empty wine bottles mother's bloody cunt master's stumpy bloody penis bangs cunt at speed woodpecker pecks. Mama's tears for a son, flats of violet pansies, rusty old shovel in Jesus' hands against master's head against master's head against master's head pop brains ooze blood against master's head pop brains ooze blood takes Suzy too long to catch up to father's newest reality: death.

Fog no longer offered JP a curtain behind which to hide. Horns honked. A fine sista rapped on JP's window. "Wake up!" She stormed off to a Rolls Royce.

He had arrived at the listening nook without any memory of driving there. That had been happening lately. Stress is what it was. His boss bullied him while colleagues snickered with their tacit approval. It was their fault; trying to mess up his retirement pension just cause they were jealous of the rumored millions he inherited from his wife's fatal fall off a mountain while hiking on their honeymoon. Office legend said he did it. They treated him like he was O.J. For that they'd all pay. He put on the earphones and pissed a river. It was warm and comfortable running down his leg.

19

"Where is she?" Chief Boggs demanded of Lake as they knelt beside Cindy's body. Lake threw a warning look at Lindsey-Smith over her shoulder.

"She's back there, Rachael. Can we leave her out of it? I don't want her involved."

"Then you shouldn't have brung her. But then that's just me." She stood.

"True, but if I followed that theory, the task force wouldn't be here now."

"You should've called for back up."

"Chief, I didn't think the tip was the real thing. That's why I came to check it out first." She stood up. "I mean, come on. Smart serials just don't suddenly go stupid and play games with the police. Not that I'm rulin out a witness leavin the tip."

"In the meantime, I don't trust writers and serials neither can help themselves."

"She writes songs." Lake's voice had grown impatient.

"People put all kinds of things in songs these days." Lake followed close on Chief Boggs' heels as she cut a path to Lindsey-Smith. "Ms Smith, one last thing, I understand you refused to make a police report. Great! Leave the bastards on the street so they can attack somebody else who might not live to tell it. That's on you, citizen." She stalked off before Lindsey-Smith could form a comeback.

So Lindsey-Smith gave Boggs the finger.

"Don't!" Lake whispered squeezing the offending finger and steering her around to face her. "You don't want any part of her. She'll win that one every time."

"She scares me." She said titillated. "But I like her."

"Not too much, I hope." Lake eyed Lindsey-Smith searching for the nasty girl and found her. "You need to stop. She's straight."

"Something's wrong with you. I couldn't begin to think like that with that poor baby...." She pointed towards the corpse. "You're jaded." Lake didn't deny it. "But then I guess you have to be."

"Sorry."

"You got nothin to apologize for." She shook her head. Maybe Lake wasn't so bad after all, even with that tin ear problem. Stop it. She was manufacturing excuses on an assembly line to stay in a questionable situation just to lick that booty. How jaded are you, Lindsey-Smith Cutter?

"You okay?"

"Hell no. If I don't stop him nobody will. This prick will keep killin. Every child he murders from here on out is on me. Hell no, I'm not okay. I'm scared. The old man said I would die if I lost. No kiddin? If I fail death's gonna be the easy way out." She placed a hand above her heart as if she was about to pledge allegiance. "I don't have the luxury of time to step inside the box and do life's little things, like make out a police report to make you cops feel better. The old man referred to a gauntlet. Last time I checked Webster's that was a race. If I'm in it I'm in it to win. Any ol thing that slows me down is on my fight me list. I don't have the luxury of time to question what's happened to me. It's as simple as that. Listen to me, Lake. We have to go back to Possum Woods."

"Shhh!" Lake stared at her incredulously. "Do you see where I am?" She waved her arms around the clearing. "C'mon, I'm not goin anywhere soon. I've got two crime sites to cover. When Doctor Perez is through with the body and the technicians finish then we investigators get our chance. You feel me? "

"*I'm* goin back to Possum Woods. All I know is, I wished for one clue. So far it aint jumped out at me. But then my memory of the whole thing is piece-meal" She kicked the dirt with the scuffed toe of her pointy cowboy boots. "Gotta do this! I'm that kind of desperate. Pieces of my memory keep breakin up into tinier pieces."

"Just in case a little advice might get through that head of yours, take care of that concussion if you want your short-term memory back any time soon."

"Alleged concussion."

"I've had a couple or three in my life. Hey, girlfriend, it's your memory and your so-called wish, which, for the record, I don't like a bit. Maybe it's the reason you don't get that I'm a police officer investigatin a child killer, the lowest quotient of humanity, the old fashion way."

"You runnin this investigation, Lieu?" Boggs shouted across the clearing.

"Speakin of...." Lieutenant Lake nodded towards the Chief.

"Then that's that." The finality of it all seemed displaced considering where they were. "What a mistake I made thinkin we came together for some higher purpose."

Silence reigned.

The drum of voices surrounding them receded into the forest.

Lake blinked. The silence cracked. "I'm not about to turn my back on this thing you have with the killer over some dyke-o-drama. We had no idea she was even missin till you came along. For that I thank you. Wish I—"

Lindsey-Smith cut her off. "Don't wish, especially anywhere near me." As if on cue a swift movement near the body attracted her. She took off running in the shadow's direction.

Stunned for a second, Lake recovered chasing after her screaming, "LINDSEY-SMITH!"

"Ms Smith, that's off limits." A freaked Chief Boggs cried out.

"Get her away from here!" Doctor Perez commanded.

Lindsey-Smith pointed at the tiny remains. "'It's mine. You....'" A jolt of electricity hit her heart like she had plugged her finger in a thunderbolt. She withdrew her finger. Cindy's last breath brushed against Lindsey-Smith's cheek.

She fainted on the corpse.

20

Lindsey-Smith bolted upright and threw a right hook. It caught a chin whose owner never saw it coming. The physical exertion ripped groans from her with claws that sank in her ribs. She hugged herself tight like a meaningful lover.

"Why am I on the cold ass ground?"

"They call me Doctor Perez." The faces said. "The coroner. Congratulations."

Her head swam in a dizzying whirlpool. "I'm dead?"

"You're my first live customer since my residency." The coroner bragged.

She squirmed as she checked to see if she was alive, attempting to sit up, she reached for a hand extended to her.

"DON'T touch! Contamination." Doctor Perez warned. "Lieutenant, you know better."

Lake threw up her hands. "Don't know what I was thinkin."

"I need your clothes, Ms Smith. They're evidence now."

In the murky water buoying her brain it almost made sense. "What's happened to me?" The outline of Lake's taunt face popped into focus, then multiplied. Red shoes came into view. Lindsey-Smith flinched.

The boots owner knelt and spoke out of all her faces. Thatched red waving above them faded pale like the Volkswagen in Possum Woods.

"Lindsey-Smith, this is Chief Boggs. I need you to listen to me. I need you to cooperate. Do you understand?"

"Yes." She mumbled although she didn't understand.

Boggs leaned uncomfortably close to her face. "Your clothes are evidence. We have to remove your clothes. Don't hit anyone else. Do you understand?"

"Shadow." She looked to Lake for help and saw that her brown uncharacteristically sympathetic eyes turned blue. Eyes of a friend.

"You fainted." Her new best friend Lake whispered unable to edit all traces of concern from her tone.

Moments later she saw double again when identical twins, one had an angry red bruise on her chin, crouched at her side. "Didn't mean to hit you." She managed. As items of clothes left her body, strangely she felt not exposed, but displayed. Cold hands that lowered her jeans brushed against more than her inner thighs. Her clitoris jumped. Her body twitched involuntarily.

"My bad." The bruised twin cooed not meaning it. She winked at Lindsey-Smith as she placed her jeans in a brown paper bag.

Lindsey-Smith had nose, she smelled her. The lady was S and M. Her injured brain cried *Get me outta here, Lake.*

"A fresh kill is the best break we didn't want." Doctor Perez said as she peered over her shoulder at the body lying beneath a towering evergreen. "It's always the tallest tree in the clearing. If he's takin souvenirs, maybe we'll find out now."

"He's takin souvenirs." Lake said knowingly. "Take a good look at her, Doc.

"I always do, Lieutenant Lake. Always do." She looked over her shoulder.

Lindsey-Smith hiccupped. "Owww."

"That hurt like hell, huh? Best I can make out you've got a few broken ribs. They'll x-ray you." Doctor Perez advised.

"Who'll x-ray me?" The doctor and Chief Boggs both looked to Lake for guidance. The next hiccup interrupted by a bad memory got caught in Lindsey-Smith's throat and almost choked her. Her brain shouted out. Pinky! They confiscated her gun. Nobody had said anything, yet. They didn't know it was real. Yet. Shit!

Her neck muscles tightened holding her in a chokehold. Her gun. Any minute somebody was going to discover it had been fired recently. She could see it, on trial for the murder of the piece of crap that tried to kill her.

"Back off Connors." Boggs' bossy voice penetrated Lindsey-Smith's panic.

"The man would steal a collar from a dog." A voice Lindsey-Smith warmed to, a whiskey flavored Alabama baritone, had arrived.

"He goes to the wall for no one." Lake tersely added. "Right, West? You know that, Chief."

"Man's a cannibal. Gonna feed him some turkey fries before he eats mine." The whiskey voice drawled.

"He's good at what he does, politics." The Chief insisted half-heartedly. "A necessary evil, Sergeant West. On the other hand Deputy Chief Connors has a nasty twist in his personality that makes him untrustworthy to socialize with on even the most minimal basis. You never know when nasty mean will show up, Sergeant, yet you can count on him showin up."

The twins helped Lindsey-Smith into a sitting position. Her black bra strap slipped off a shoulder. That Connors dude sounded like a piece of work. Fortunately, he wasn't her concern.

"How'd the caller, whoever he was, get your cell phone number?" Boggs questioned Lieutenant Lake.

"Tons of people have my card. I give it to witnesses and victims in case they need to reach me."

"In case he calls again I'm gonna have the FBI put a trace on all calls to your phone, which I'm sure he expects. It'll turn out he's usin a throwaway cell. He's smart."

"He didn't sound white, black, or Hispanic." Lindsey-Smith heard Lake making it up. "Course that doesn't really work anymore. Some of us sound white. Some blacks and some whites are Hispanic. Some whites sound black." She addressed the last remark to West.

"Watch it now." He hitched up his droopy pants and face.

Lindsey-Smith saw that West was a middle-aged hefty man with stooped shoulders and a hound dogface. She reminded herself to remember how easily Lake lied. And then forgot. A cell phone chimed too sweetly lending macabre harmonics to the score, and along came the memory of the phone that Lake told her to toss. They've got those pieces. Should she try to get them back? No that would attract attention. Chill, the phone's broken. They have zero reasons to put it back together. She was convinced.

"I'm better now. I think I can stand."

Lake stepped between the twin with the yen and Lindsey-Smith, grabbing her arm to lend support, "I've got her." She waited until the twins were out of earshot, "She could just eat your cookie up." Lindsey-Smith didn't hear her.

A shiver ran through her as she stared beyond the trees to where the shadow's trapezoidal heads slipped between darkness and light. The M.E. draped a white cotton sheet on her shoulders and like a shroud it slid around her body.

21

Not a word passed between the two women until they took a dogleg path to the right through the woods a mile away from the crime scene. An innocent shadow struck at Lindsey-Smith's head. She ducked.

Lake lowered her flashlight beam. "Why'd you duck?"

"I didn't duck."

"Sure you did. Like—," she ducked her head to the left, "—that."

Lindsey-Smith felt Lake's eyes rake over her, suspicions mounting into questions, and theories, the cop in her. She quickened her pace any ol way hurting or not.

"The coroner says the girl died around midnight." Lindsey-Smith suspected there was a question in that statement, if so she left it alone. "You hit the time on the head. At least we know his watch had the right time. Who is he?"

"Who cares? How do I wipe his planet out? That's what I wanna know."

"I don't condone murder."

"He does. Trust me. It doesn't matter what you condone. You're walkin too fast again. Can't take deep breaths. God, that hurts." She hobbled on.

"You should've waited for the ambulance, damn dykes." Lights from TV news' vans trickled through the trees. "Vultures! Bout time they started showin up."

"One of those vultures followed me—"

Lake cut her off, "Don't talk to them!"

"Somebody needs to tell them bout themselves." Lake turned around and shone the flashlight in Lindsey-Smith's eyes. She shoved it aside. "Don't do that. I'm already seein double."

"You need to understand. Basically, media doesn't give a damn bout kids of color. If we had more coverage, just an iota of what they put out for wealthy white kids we'd make it harder for this scum to operate. Right now he's fuckin invisible. Totally off the radar of the general public."

Lindsey-Smith tugged at Lake's sleeve. "Except for *The Defender*, my sister's kidnappin didn't even make the papers. But every where I looked there were pictures of this rich blond blue eye girl who went missin a year before my baby sister." She halted. "What made her more special than my sister? I hated that little girl. I hoped they never found her. That was terrible wasn't it, to wish something like that?"

Lake urged her ahead with the flashlight beam. Lindsey-Smith had never told a soul about those twisted childhood thoughts that now soured on her lips. They marched down a path that had widened enough for them to walk side-by-side. A sliver of moonlight cut across her face making it appear slashed. "My brain's tryin to remember something that just won't stick around long enough for me to catch."

"When the swellin goes down your short term memory will return. In the meantime, taint nothin you can do except drive yourself crazy tryin to remember something that might not even be there."

"Easy for you to say you're wearin clothes."

"Which reminds me. Before you passed out you said, 'It's mine.'"

She stopped in her tracks, "It's mine? That's it, 'it's mine'. That's what the prick kept repeatin over and over. 'It's mine.' Actually, he didn't speak with his mouth. It all went down in his head. He lives in his head. At least he can trust his brain." She paused, and struggled with it while Lake waited impatiently. They walked under the lights of the parking lot. "Say something."

"You heard what he thought? C'mon. That's a little rich don't you think?" She didn't wait for an answer. "Gotta get back. Lindsey. Really, I hate to leave you hangin after what all you been through. Go take care of yourself. Straighten your head out."

A black panel van rolled under a street lamp catching Lindsey-Smith's eye before it pulled out of the light. "I'm missin pieces, Lake. I need down time so I can think. I can't fuckin think." She wanted to grab her head, hold the pieces in, but her ribcage would take a bite out of her ass if she tried. "Scan this. I'm pullin my hair out."

"I should be the one pullin my weave out. Up in flames goes my fifteen year career and law degree. That's eighty-five percent of my life." Lake grumbled as she ducked under yellow police tape.

"That's not a weave."

"I'm just sayin." She sighed away the frustration.

The two women, one wrapped in a white shroud, broke for the waiting ambulance ahead of reporters and camera crews that bum rushed them.

As she ducked into the back of the ambulance, Lindsey-Smith whispered to the lieutenant, "You believe."

"Only what I can see." The doors swung shut.

22

Inside the black van JP raged as he involuntarily turkey-necked on each word, "Who...are...you? Who...are...you, cunt?" No mas. He wasn't going to ask that question again.

She had invaded his mind. "It's mine." His soprano voice shouted. The woman would have no way of knowing his ritual unless she was there when he thought it like she said. "How is that possible? A tip my ass? I put that witness to sleep. I did. MEEE, muthafucka. Nobody left a tip, Lieutenant Lyin-ass Lake."

He slammed his foot on the gas pedal, whipped a right into a brightly lighted gas station, a left out of it, and west after the rapist riding in the ambulance. He got in line behind a news' van following the ambulance and quickly found a better plan. Lieutenant Lake had directed the ambulance to Stroger's Hospital.

He peeled off the news van's tail.

He peeled off his latex gloves.

He peeled open his fly and fucked the idea like he hated it until he exploded across his windshield.

In his mind he stayed in hot pursuit.

23

10:03 pm. Halloween. PCH. Sixty mile per hour gusts buffeted the swerving orange Corvette shoving it sideways, dangerously close to the mountainside while sheets of horizontal rain slowed its upward journey to a wet cat creeping in the dark on a moonless night.

On the other side of the mountain, a half-mile behind the catty Corvette, a winding tail of car lights twinkled and twitched in the dark. Without caution, the cat's tail ascended into obsidian, a seamless merger of horizon and sky.

Lightening bolts zipped open the night and exposed the other side of day.

Hell's fireball gates imploded open. Beastly minions cheered to a cacophony that shattered eardrums. Jagged flashes of electricity clapped. Thunder beat out a tympanic fanfare roll for the procession up the twisting mountain.

And bullying rain turned car roofs into beat boxes.

"Where you at, Orange? I wanna tap that butt." Dracula teased. "I should've won the costume contest. Nobody sacrificed more than me. Plucked out my fuckin eyes."

"Cept the man who beheaded himself," asserted Swan Neck who had no face. Lightening flared over the Corvette. She pointed. "Get her soul!"

Satan laughed.

It knocked a Hummer-size tooth from a peak that smashed into cars knocking several over the mountain into the Pacific Ocean. The Mercedes braked. Spun out, and then went airborne.

24

"Be careful of what you wish for." Satan warned slyly. "Condemnment three."

"That is the premise of their propositions," Satan's human mentor pointed at the earth, down through the clouds at heads on PCH and in Chicago. He cheesed proudly.

"Pride never understands that condemnment three is a perfect triangle." Satan warned as his terrible gaze returned to his beloved earth. "You just might get it."

25

From a dark place inside a warped sleep Lindsey-Smith felt the piercing glare of beady eyes boring holes in her forehead, the legless man. A hand gripped her shoulder.

"Hey, lady, you're not supposed to sleep too long."

She yawned. It hurt bad enough to swear off yawning for life. Her blurred vision settled on IV tubes leading into her left arm. She got up and slurred into a dead swoon. Lake caught her.

"I'm okay. Not really. Did you find Cindy's mom?" There was desperation in her voice that had never been there before.

"It may take awhile. We're lookin for the identity of two girls."

She carefully rolled her eyes around to the hand on her shoulder that wanted to make it better. "What time is it?"

Lake checked her Timex. "A little after six. We need to do this now.... Get you dressed, you know cause I'm dead on my feet. The way I'm feelin if somebody was to piss me off I'd shoot em. I don't have the energy to communicate any other way." Lindsey-Smith raised the arm hooked up to IVs. "Right." Lake rang for help.

"Have you ever broken a rib?"

"My ankle. Tripped over a crack in the sidewalk. No shit."

Suppressed laughter almost ripped out her chest. And the damn Ace Bandage encircling her torso itched. "I'm goin to love this." She scratched at the bandage. "Feels like I'm wearin Itchy and Scratchy."

"Take the pain prescription. Your doctor says you refused it." She followed Lindsey-Smith's eyes as they scanned the room. "Lookin for something?"

"A mirror."

They both checked out the room: square blood red contamination trash can, beige boxes of surgical gloves, graphic posters of the heart and lungs on the walls, a mirror. Lake retrieved it.

"Doctor Simone said your plastic surgery's healin nicely. No harm came to it."

Lindsey-Smith's breath caught in her throat when she saw her blackened eyes nearly swollen shut peering back at her. A golf ball on her temple with butterfly stitches crowned the effect. Stitches on a mauled cheek and a purple cherry on her bottom lip added to the ruin that had become her face. Suddenly, she truly understood what that meant. No more tossin aside complements on her complexion. A statuesque nurse with a salt and pepper natural blew in and disconnected her from IVs. "Now what, I have no clothes?" Lake had already zipped open a backpack and pulled out a cardigan sweater.

"What? You look relieved. Admit it. You thought I brought you girly clothes. Don't lie." She teased as she slid a sleeve over Lindsey-Smith's arm.

"Actually, I thought I had to pull it over my head."

"You think I'm cruel. Or thoughtless. Try bendin your arms, rather than lettin them dangle. Did you notice if he wore a ring?"

"I don't know. Don't think so." She examined her hands. "Ouch!"

"When you left home this mornin this didn't hurt."

"Ouch. I looked different, too." She gritted her teeth against the pain. "I think the girl called for her mother. How is it possible that none of the mothers have contributed something you can use?"

Lake placed a finger on Lindsey-Smith's lips. "Not one crack ho has a mind left by the time we find her. Worst than your short term memory loss, they had nothin. By sponsorin their crack binges he neutralizes them. Lays out big bucks to do it, too. Practically outright buys the girls. The hos get so high they forget they've got a kid. That lessens the possibility of early discovery, which decreases the possibility that trace evidence will survive. Put your leg in. Could you see his fingers through the gloves? Did they have a scar on em? Anything identifiable?" She lay off when she saw the faraway look in Lindsey-Smith's eyes.

"'It's mine. You can't have it, Cindy.'" She grabbed Lake's hands. "That's what he kept repeatin super fast. So fast it...." Her train of thought entered a tunnel.

"So fast it what?"

"Sounds like he's chantin, 'It's mine. You can't have it, Cindy.' Baby, get me out of here!" She shuffled into the busy ER corridor where patients on gurneys and in wheelchairs overflowed. A pudgy old white guy in dollar store sunglasses looked up and down the corridor and past her before turning and limping off on an aluminum cane.

In his possession the man had the mother of all tools—rage, enticed by the weight of a gun under his Brown Elephant cashmere sweater. As his loafers stepped towards the ER doors he felt a malevolent presence pierce his back between the shoulder blades.

His finger tightened around the trigger. "You can't have my words, cunt." He aimed his body in the two women's direction.

The salt and pepper coiffed nurse broke through the doors pushing a wheelchair with a woman in labor. They jostled him aside. Another wave of injured followed accompanied by Chicago's Finest. His brain unscrambled. He changed directions.

The ER doors closed behind JP.

26

As Lake's department issued Crown Victoria sped onto Lake Shore Drive heading south into morning rush hour traffic Lindsey-Smith decided against going home.

"Take me to my parents' house. Go out the drive. They're closer to your place, you know. While my dad's out of town I can use the Range Rover."

"By the way, if you look out your window you'll see that we're on The Drive. How's that ride?"

"Like a crack addict on gas." She squeezed out through clinched teeth pushing back at the pothole the car hit. Going home didn't even come into play. Not while Jason Banks waited impatiently for her in a white-on-white world that the human eye couldn't see. So why was the psycho able to see it? The reason might not even be important in the scheme of things. Hey, a better question would be: how did she see through his eyes?

Lake exited at McCormick Place. "You're goin back to Possum Woods." She said accusingly.

"Jason's connected to your investigation, you know."

"You can't know that without hard evidence."

"*You* need hard evidence. I've got something better, in case you didn't notice."

"That's you. If I want to stay on this case, I can't find Banks' body. Yes, I want to keep my job. I stop pedophiles from hurtin children. Fifteen. That's how many I've taken down. How bout you?"

"No matter how hard you cops work on catchin this monster you won't. If I don't stop him nobody will. That's the deal."

"That's the difference in professionals and amateurs. We

68

have to go on to stop the next killer. And there's always another one. Havin said that, you're the best bet we've got right now. I hate sayin it but there it is. Till this thing happened to you we had all of nothin. Still, reconsider takin something for pain. The agony you're in is hangin out all over your face."

"Do you think?"

"You know what I mean." And she turned her attention to Lake Michigan where the rising sun painted the slick slate surface with yellows and fire.

"Do you have a substance abuse problem?" She steered the Mustang into the far left lane.

"Why would you go there? Oh, that's right, you're a detective."

"You screw your face up every time I mention takin pain pills."

She spat out, "Next exit." Then curtly gave her parents' address.

"Nice address." The Mustang took the curving exit on two wheels.

Lindsey-Smith pressed an imaginary brake. "So what is it bout me that makes you ask me if I'm an addict? I mean you could've asked if I've got allergies. Or how bout...." She let her voice trail. It came back on the other side of her world. "Maybe a bad thing happened when I was twelve cause a pit pull attacked me and my mother saved my life and almost lost hers. And the good doctor at Cook County filled my little body with a lot of pain medication. So much that I let a pervert steal my lil sister almost from my arms." A sigh filled with the lost breath of murdered children replaced the car's air.

Lake lowered the top. "What happened?"

"It's a story."

"You're lyin, girlfriend. You wouldn't play with something like that."

"I don't remember most of it." She avoided looking into the sun as it peeked over the horizon. Stars no longer twinkled in the big city. But the sun's shine had never dulled. "Over time, the story came out of a need to fill in the blanks. I figured it must've happened something like that. I was the only witness. Of course I was. And messed up on drugs." Her fists clenched.

The childish outburst welled up inside her bursting against her better judgment to be still, the better to hear the faint rumblings of an ancient memory tumbling down from darkness between bodies of innocents. She over responded. "I bet you interrogate all your dates."

"Everybody's got an occupational habit. Like you writers, you embellish everything." The Mustang hit the South Loop traveling sixty swishing by Soldiers Field—the Monster on the Midway—a corn on the Field Museum's white dinosaur feet.

As they traveled west on Roosevelt Road, the south alley of the Magnificent Mile, Lindsey-Smith watched the backside of the loop slip by and had a change of heart. "This is gonna get heavy real fast if you can't ask me a simple question without taggin it with a suspicion. 'Do you do drugs?' Not a problem. I'd answer that question anytime. But the question assumes the worst bout me? I don't know bout other women you dated, but accusatory questions turn me off. And I don't have an on switch. But I get it. It's your nature. Tellin stories is mine. We can't help it even if we want to. It's like bein a domesticated animal. Or not. *Or not* one day will bite you in the ass or on the neck if you're a gay Las Vegas star. There's the house."

"You can train a tiger. You just can't train it not to kill." Her BlackBerry vibrated. "Lake!" After a minute as she disconnected she grabbed the seat belt. "Put that back on."

"Excuse me." Half out half in the car she glared at Lake.

"Swats on its way to bust a crack house. Cindy's mother might be inside."

She clunked back in the seat forgetting about Justin Banks. "That was fast. What's up?"

"The Amber Alert and that funny money the killer lays on em. Apparently a sista tried to buy crack with a wad of nineteen eighty-seven twenties. The dealers thought she was passin counterfeit paper. Seems they were too young to remember the old currency. Shots were fired. Tried to kill her I guess. May have for all we know at this point."

"And I get to go with you?"

"I'm stashin you in a squad car outside the perimeter. Seat belt! Not lettin you out of my eyesight."

"How will that play with your boss?"

"She won't know. Right? One of us needs to pick up a couple of throwaways. I don't want the FBI listenin in on our conversations."

She watched Lake slip into deep thought. "Maybe that excuse for a woman knows something that might help jog my memory. I'm desperate." Her head swam. *Anything'll do, baby* played on a track in her brain that had nothing to do with the moment. First a loser's song, now a pity me love song had come to nest. Career screwed was due up next.

27

To avoid familiarity JP never ordered the same breakfast twice at the corner Foodie Grill, a throwback greasy spoon with a row of orange pleather counter stools on rusting chrome pedestals where four diners hunkered down slurping coffee.

His preference, the privacy of the high-back booths of which there were two. A Goth couple barely out of their teens occupied the booth by the door. JP's favorite.

JP remembered to smile. "Halloween was yesterday."

The Marilyn Manson wanna-be leaped into his insulter's face. "Fuck off, Republican!" He snorted.

Not to be messed with, JP played the ace up his sleeve. He fanned a flush, five crisp new twenty-dollar bills, in the boy-of-many piercings' face. "This hand for this booth." He placed the cash on the table in front of the girl-of-many tattoos.

"God bless you!" The couple marveled in unison, and then jetted from the grill.

He didn't see that coming. JP had taken off a half day from work to close on his last piece of property. With the check already in an off shore bank, he felt like celebrating with the one thing he enjoyed, a great meal. He sucked on a juicy lemon slice plucked from the Goth's saucer. The back of his jaws ached. His mouth watered. "Nice."

A twitchy bleached blond waif sidled up to the man's booth and inquired anxiously, "You hungry today?" He nodded. She shot a snaggletooth smile over her order pad. "Twice in one week. People might say you taken a likin to Danny's cookin."

The man remembered to smile. "How's Zoenommy?"

"She's good. Wow! You remember how to say her name after hearin it one time."

"Love the way it sounds. Makes it easy to remember."

"You're real unusual."

The man placed his order. "Six sunny side up. Ten slices of bacon. Chorizo. Four blueberry pancakes. Grits. O.J. Black coffee. Big bowl."

Seven minutes later he piled everything together in the big bowl, poured coffee and OJ over it, and topped it off with maple syrup. Within minutes the bowl gleamed.

As men went JP was aware he was shorter than average and thinner than he preferred, but malnutrition in childhood had lead to an adult body that could never eat enough. He wiped his pink lips with a napkin and crumbled it into the plate. In his black marble eyes glaring lights turned on and replaced the black pupils.

The waitress slid the check in front of the man. "Anybody ever tell you that you got eyes like Jim Lehrer? You know that old dude on channel eleven." She quivered.

JP slapped two twenties on the table and adjusted a silk candy stripe tie flattening it against a charcoal shirt. "Time to go to work." He stood. "Win anything on those lottery tix I gave you?"

"Nothin. But Zoenommy plays with em. It really helps with her math homework like you said. I like you cause you're very informational. See you."

"Yes, you will."

2-8

At seven forty a.m., as rare as cul-de-sacs were in Chicago, the bust went down in one. The street yelled unyielding poverty, hopelessness, and crime through boarded up windows where a half-century before proud curtains fluttered.

Streets sparkled with broken glass, blushed with cigarette butts, and cried with people hanging on corners and off sagging front porches; cell phones brazenly photographed police. Blue and whites blocked off two square blocks surrounding the cul-de-sac.

With a story fit for a scam artist Lindsey-Smith conned her way out of the squad car. Into an alley and over the first backyard fence she jumped. Over a rickety wood fence she climbed, over the last, a cyclone fence, she landed in the dog house and collapsed the roof with bold red letters that spelled: SATAN. She ran. Ran until she plastered her back against the exposed clapboards of a frame house where she positioned herself to gain an angled view of Chief Boggs and Lake crouched on the driver's side of the Chief's gray unmarked. Behind them, on the east side of the street, the shadow appeared on the roof of a four-story apartment building.

Over the shadow's wide shoulders the rising sun dissolved into morning light that spit fire and exploded sharply. Almost simultaneously Rachael Boggs' body slammed against her car and slid off.

Lake flung her body on top of the Chief.

For a dizzying heartbeat Lindsey-Smith didn't connect the dots. When she did the sun exploded again. Bullets punched holes in the gray car above Lake's head. To Lindsey-Smith's horror she realized that the shooter was finding his range even as Lake fired blindly into the sun's glare. Down the block two swat officers firing their weapons at the shooter ran towards the pinned women.

Unaffected the shooter continued to fire. And only Lindsey-Smith had the angle to see why he was unaffected. She glimpsed a disorienting reflection meant to confuse shooters returning fire. "Lake, shoot at the center of the sun! The center of the sun, SHOOOT!" A mirror shattered flinging shards at the sun and off the roof with the cart wheeling shooter. She squeezed her eyes shut just before his head smacked the concrete.

Shouts for an ambulance pried open her eyes. Lake, splashed in her ex-lover's blood, administered CPR.

"Save her, Lake. Please please." Lindsey-Smith whispered, feeling lightheaded, and surprised at how sick she felt when she thought Lake might be killed. After several shallow breaths she collapsed against the house. "Damn me." Her obsession with the shadow had almost killed Lake. An acrid sweet odor sprung up around her. Her twitching nose guided her eyes to her feet where a sliver of light broke through a gapping hole in the deteriorating gangway pavement. Intuitively, she shifted her feet away from the light.

The sidewalk collapsed.

She fell towards the blade of light, an incandescent bulb dangling from the basement ceiling. A big tobacco brown fist wielding a twelve-inch butcher knife charged her. Stunned by the fall her body refused to get off her spread-eagle butt. Even when bloodshot eyes curiously stared down at her. Even when the knife plunged towards her chest. It nailed her sweater to the dirt floor. Ribcage pain nailed her heart. Her right hand touched a gooey gummy mass. She clutched a handful and heaved it into the red eyes. The man of the house dropped the knife as he scrambled backwards shaking his head and furiously wiping his face.

The low wattage bulb cast its light through an old wood crate leaving bars of alternating light and shadow across the man's face. Either he was in prison or she was. The answer bought her kicking and flailing to her feet.

"Mister! I fell in. That didn't come out right. What I'm sayin is...uh, I didn't break in. Believe me. Those police out there, they aren't after me...."

When she mentioned the police she notice that he stared up at the hole through which she fell. He should have been pissed, but the bugged out eyes said he was scared shitless.

"That's not it is it, Mister?" Lake's slip-on Bjorns stuck to a sticky mass as she stepped back into just enough light to see the knife sticking up in the dirt.

They both launched for it.

On a scale of one to ten Lindsey-Smith's ribcage pain hit infinity when the man's weight slammed on top of her. In his grasp the terrible butcher knife, the biggest one she had ever seen, stopped threatening to kill her. The man clutched it to his chest. You win came to her mind and was greeted by a gurgling sound that emanated from the man as he slumped over on his face, his rear end stuck up in the air. Her head shook in denial, her mouth mumbled pitifully, "Please don't be dead. God, I killed a poor man tryin to defend his home. I am seriously fucked."

Before she could scream arms wrapped around her neck; a bony face pressed against hers dislodging the bandage on her cheek. "Get away from me!" She flung the arms from her neck and suffered for it. "Who are you, woman?"

"You my shero. My shero." The emaciated woman cried then pointed to the dead man, when she did she hit the light bulb. It swung crazily casting light on her chicken neck where Lindsey-Smith made out a thin line of oozing red ruby beads. Embarrassed, the woman wiped away blood smearing it across her throat. "He was gonna cut my head off."

The face above the smear Lindsey-Smith noted was that of an old woman with what was left of a young life adorned with eyes that she would know anywhere. Cindy's last breath brushed against her cheek. "Cindy," stumbled from her mouth. She already regretted the indiscretion.

"My baby?" The skeleton asked suspicion backing her off

on shaky legs. "Where's Cindy? Why you lookin at me like that?"

She stepped towards the bag of bones. "Look, I'm sorry." That sticky stuff pulled at her shoe. A putrid stench overwhelmed her guts. But she stepped up and extended her hand. The light flickered. In spite of it, she knew a decapitated head when she saw it... saw them...lots of them in various stages of decomposition.

For a split second she stared at her suddenly foreign right hand before madly scraping the palm against the crate.

29

The newly formed Special Task Force Headquarters was located in a new state of the art beige brick three-level building on the northwest side at the top of a slight incline that over looked Elston Avenue on the mostly Latino auto body shop strip.

Lieutenant Lake adjusted her hip holster then opened the front door with a keycard and disappeared inside.

She plopped down in an office chair in front of a five-foot long mahogany desk. When her butt hit the chair it rolled back a foot on a brown concrete floor. Uncomfortable in the rolling chair, the Lieutenant leaped to her feet. On solid ground, "Why are we in Boggs' office?" Her eyes slanted as they scrutinized the desk and office for changes.

"That's a problem that little friendship between Boggs and you." Deputy Chief Connors, his back to the window, stood rigid, royalty overlooking its fiefdom. Lake's nostrils flared. Connors pivoted around and turned the monitor on his desk to face her, from it Lindsey-Smith's face, wrinkled nose and all, stared back at her.

Lake's complexion toasted with anger.

"She's been at three separate crime scenes. Why did Boggs tolerate that?" He asked rhetorically. "Your friendship. If it gets out, this task force is in trouble. The press, the politicians who didn't want this department's expense, will do anything; they'll do anything to destroy this department. I'll do what I have to, to keep it."

"What do you want, a metal and a chest to stick it on?" She turned the monitor to face him. "I make no apologies for havin a life. She brought down a serial that we didn't even know existed. You can't put that on her doorstep. It's on us that we didn't know the fuck ass was out there takin heads. A civilian did our job. Do you really want the press to muck around in those waters?"

"They already are."

"Well there you go." She planted her hands palm down on the desk. "You need a sacrificial lamb. My woman, yeah I said it, she aint your goat. She aint it. I've known you fifteen years, Jack. I've got your number and your address. I know where to FED EX the bullshit."

"Return to sender. You don't scare me."

"Then you're a bigger fool than I thought you were. And in my mind, I've always thought you took the gold metal in the fool's event. Touch her and this cold war turns hot." She stood up. "I'm the dyke that made you look bad in the academy and I'll make you look bad in your grave if you fuck with Lindsey, Jack."

"Last I noticed the academy was sixteen years of yesterdays. To...today I'm your boss." Lake smacked the desk and turned to leave. "Superintendent Smith heard from reliable sources that your piece of trim—" Lake spun around to face him, "—keeps sho...showin up on crime sc...sc...sc...scenes and that she took a pratfall on the first fresh body we've had in twelve, er thirteen, homicides. If the press gets wind of this, and you know they will...well, you see how bad that looks for us. And that's a problem, Kyniska. My problem until Rachael returns." He grinned sparingly. "What do you think I should do with you?" Jilted by an urgent rap on the door he stood down. Their eyes locked across the desk. The raps on the door returned harder.

30

Brilliant mid-day sunlight sliced through bare tree branches and splashed on the roof of the pale red Volkswagen as Lindsey-Smith peered into the passenger side window noting keys in the ignition, a pale blue CUBS' cap on the passenger seat, lemon mentholated throat lozenges in a tin, and a dead man in the passenger seat.

She tweaked her chin. And wondered why she felt compelled to come back? To look around again, the obvious. The old man called it proof. Proof of what? Was it proof that Cindy was a real person and her murder just as real? Proof. Got it, girl? Nothing more and nothing less. In case she was wrong she surveyed the car and body one last time.

As she turned to leave an anaconda tightened around her chest, paranoia seized her common sense. She looked down at her tracks, lots of tracks, not just hers. A sharp pain deep inside her head stabbed her sticky reasoning. Her tracks were distinctive. The Bjorns had been given up as evidence. Bare footed, she had picked up a pair of knock off Crocs from a twenty-four hour drug store, the only place selling shoes at that time of the morning. The officers who took her home observed her make the purchase.

With an evergreen branch she obliterated her tracks. As she backed out of the road she nearly stepped on a mound of dirt with odd symbols, odd because they shouldn't have been in the woods all by themselves. The symbols began with a backwards S followed by: *A # : sol*

She ran a hand over her hair. "You make these?" She asked the dead man. A familiar shadow spread across her face.

31

The cold interrogation room, its discomfort level ran high by design, a two way mirror, and the gray concrete slab walls, the poured concrete floor. A metal table, four feet by four feet, seperated Lieutenant Lake from the walking dead in Brenda Patron's sunken eyes. She had been told about her daughter Cindy. Her dehydrated lips smacked together. "Her name's not Cindy." She whimpered. "Cinderella, that's what I named her." The blistered sores on Patron's face rearranged themselves.

Lake, leaning over the addict, spoke quietly without inflexion. "You said you wouldn't talk to anybody else but me. Talk to me, Brenda. I'm here."

"They said you know my shero. She knows Cinderella, too. Can I talk to her?"

"Here's the deal. Answer my questions and I'll set up a meet with your shero. How's that sound, Brenda? I'll bring her here. Right here in this room." She glared at the two-way mirror. "Aint that right, Connors?" She returned her attention to Patron. "You with me?"

Patron's gaming eyes searched Lake's unsympathetic eyes for a trick.

"My shero's gonna make that bastard pay for hurtin my Cinderella."

"She's not a police officer, Brenda."

"Police officers didn't save my life."

Four hours later, the Lieutenant narrowed her cat eyes on the two-way mirror. After a stiff moment she stalked to a control panel located on the wall by the door and ended the audio-video recording of the interview.

In the beige hallway outside interrogation room four, the

number painted with black block lettering, Lake, with one Frye boot propped against the wall, leaned back against it and rested.

Connors struck a military bearing during his introduction of Assistant District Attorney, Carry Mellon.

"We're gonna arraign Patron." The ADA informed Lake in a tone that made it explicit—there was no room for debate.

Lake pushed away from the wall. "What's the hurry? The longer we wait to question Patron the sicker she gets. In an hour all she'll be thinkin bout is gettin well."

Connors stuck his chin in the ring. "The public needs to know we're makin every effort to catch this...this...preference offender."

The tapetum, the reflective eye layer that glows in the dark in cats' eyes, blazed in Lake's. She pushed back. "Brenda Patron is the soberest mother we've had to date. Right now, her memory's slidin down the mountainside faster than an avalanche. I'm not lettin her go until she bottoms out."

"She's already there." The ADA opined.

"And you know that how?" Lake asked patronizingly.

"It's not like the ho's goin anywhere." Connors snapped with finality. "Bitch will never make the one mil bail Carry's goin to ask for."

"I'll get it, too. She bartered her little girl for a fix. We're sendin a message." Sergeant West cleared his throat as he approached the threesome.

"We're busy, Sergeant." Connors pointed out.

"Yeah. Lieu, we've ID'd Angel Doe. Latissa," he checked a BlackBerry, "Naw, Catissa Waters. Seven years old. The mother OD'd last Halloween, befo she got round to reportin her missin." West trumpeted. His hound dog eyes rolled at Connors.

"Inquiries?"

"No, Lieu. Aint nobody missin her. We backed into it from school records. She never returned after Halloween last year. No record of a transfer. Teacher didn't miss her. Too many kids comin and goin all semester long. Transfers don't git noticed, as a result." His face drooped. "Cryin shame aint it. This Halloween thing, we seein a pattern here?"

The BlackBerry inside Lake's wool jacket pocket vibrated. She answered, "Lieutenant Lake!" It was a quick conversation, a terrible conversation that stretched across her taunt face. Her voice slid into morose tones when she uttered, "Chief Boggs died at four-forty."

32

The HD plasma in Lindsey-Smith's studio office nestled neatly in a corner near her glass desk, for the third time, played the video recording of Patron's interrogation. Several of the things said about the killer resonated.

Patron's mouth turns down. "He's Chicano like me."

On that statement Lake strolled into the office. "He's a chameleon. Better than any I've ever seen. Black mothers describe him as African-American. Latin mothers say he's Latino. White hos say he's white; one said skinhead without the tatts." She sighed.

"I'm sorry about Chief Boggs. I didn't know you two were ex-lovers." She saw a tear puddle in Lake's penetrating eyes.

"Leave it alone." She immediately raised an apologetic hand. "No. I'm really not that kind of a bitch. It sounds like I'm attackin you for bein sympathetic." To ward off a response she hurried along. "Disguise artists are the hardest perps to catch because we don't know what they look like. I'm spendin the night. Do what you want with that." She made a yawning getaway unnoticed by the preoccupied Lindsey-Smith who pushed fast forward on the remote.

"You sold your baby," Lieutenant Lake shouts at Brenda Patron.

"Nooo! Mia nina." Brenda screams. Hysteria takes over.

Lake slaps the woman so hard her head bobbles. "You were supposed to keep her safe. Now pull yourself together. Help us revenge her death."

To Lindsey-Smith Brenda Patron's face defined living breathing chaos. And her eyes defined trapped, only able to dart around the room looking for a way out it. Trapped eyes resonated with the wishscapes.

"He gave Cinderella lottery tickets outside Sweets Candy Store. She didn't win. But he gave her money to feel better. She bought the money home to me. A hundred dollars in funny lookin twenties. He...she said he liked her name. No wait. He liked the sound of her name. That was real weird. Cinderella didn't like people callin her Cindy. It was too plain for her. Can I see my baby?"

"What did you say?"

Reverse. Play.

"He...she said he liked her name. No wait. He liked the sound of her name."

Reverse. Play.

"He liked the sound of her name."

Lindsey-Smith noticed that Patron's jaws slid back and forth chewing on gum that wasn't there, fiending. She needed a fix.

"He's a shorty. Where's my baby? Where's my Cinderella."

Lindsey-Smith punched the pause button. She assumed the *Thinkers* pose. The ol man had said if she didn't accept the wish they'd be screwed like Cinderella after midnight. Two mentionings of Cinderella couldn't be a coincidence. She turned to Lake for an answer. "Lake!" She called. "Where you at?" Never mind.

She cocked her head. Sadly, she didn't know the names of eleven of the murdered girls. Nor did she know what they looked like. That was something she planned to remedy ASAP, first thing in the morning. In the meantime, she was left with a nagging question, *what's in a name?* "Lake!" She turned off the TV, and then pulled herself off the chair. "Lake!"

33

Brenda Patron made her way down an alley—where a family of burly rats tugged at a slice of pizza with a cigarette stubbed out in the cheese.

Luck, she thought busted her out of jail. Nobody she knew had the kind of money that it took to post her bail. Jailers must have gotten her mixed up with somebody she reasoned. Right now she needed a bump.

She heard shuffling noises behind her. When she looked over her shoulder she saw a rat scattering with the pizza into a hole under a wood fence. That's when Patron made the decision. She would kill herself, but not before the police caught the pervert that hurt her baby. When it came time for her to testify maybe she could slip a knife into court.

A mental note formed a bubble above her head that said tell that detective lady about the sucker he gave Cinderella. It looked just like her.

"Cinderella." It crushed every bone in her chest. If she lived to be hundred, which she wouldn't, the bones would never mend.

A hand grabbed her hair and forced her head forward. It was at that moment that she knew who bailed her out.

Brenda Patron was only five feet two and eighty-five pounds, yet an ass kicking street fighter from the day she was born on 48th and South Ugly Street in the backseat of a jitney cab.

Instinctively, knowing she had seconds to live she forced her jagged dirty fingernails through latex gloves.

34

Recessed lights in the blue-gray ceiling gave the master bedroom a soft glow. A teak queen-size sleigh bed, its bedding laid in a black and white print of women's faces during orgasms, owned the middle of the room. Above, a skylight opened up the room to constellations.

Lindsey-Smith, wet from a shower, pulled back the bedcovers exposing sumptuous rump, round and firm and she lowered her head and she smooched the crack were it curved into pubic hairs glistening in cootchie juice. Catching a drop on her tongue she rolled it around tasting Lake's recipe: salt, honey, lime, hazel nut and savory of pussy. She accepted the invitation. As she stroked the envelope her grinding pelvis spooned against Lake's burning booty, which answered in slow grinding thrusts that parted her creamed lips tickling and enticing her lover's fingertips until they slid on top and played with Lake's jumpin clit. The lieutenant clamped her thighs around Lindsey-Smith's hand grinding her stuff like she wanted to tear it up.

Two minutes into it Lake pumped out a begging orgasm, "Suck me like you hate me." She snatched Lindsey-Smith on top of her and shoved her head down. Half way she jerked Lindsey-Smith up and hugged her so tight she cried uncle. Lake cautioned, "Shhh!" Her voice deepened. Her throaty moans snatched Lindsey-Smith's pussy sideways. She lost all connection with the world beyond Lake's soft wet mouth.

Their tongues entwined explored and made nasty girl promises.

Lindsey-Smith slammed her pelvic against flickering fingers sassing her clit.

"I could hurt that pussy if you don't let me calm it down." Like a long silk scarf Lake slid between her thighs.

Lindsey-Smith swooned. Shame on me she scolded herself as if she could control where she was headed feeling Lake's long fingers ease inside her gaping round looking for the cherry in all the right places. Like all dykes she can't wait to stick it in there. Let's see what she's got. She arched her back and raised her hips onto Lake's fingers forcing them in deeper. Then her virgina squeezed Lake's fingers massaging them, and when they rammed, her pussy muscles expelled them from her pot of cream.

Lake's hand trembled when she laid her middle finger on the rim of her round and her bitch sucked it inside. Her hot mouth wrapped around Lindsey-Smith's nipple as she pummeled her walls plucking all the cherries until her pussy vibrated coming shamelessly.

"Sweet Jesus, you got that lesbian pussy."

"How many you got in? Shit! Fuck me with all of 'em. Hit that pussy with your pistol, daddy. To the right. To the right. Hit it, bitch like you fuckin mean it. Daddy. DADDY. DADDYYYYY. Da'mnnnnn it's been so long. So long." She came five times in minutes too short to count. And a screamer like she'd never been before.

Bam! Lindsey-Smith felt the startling heat of Lake's mouth wrap around her swollen clit and roll it back and forth suck back and forth suck back and forth suck strutting with her pistol squishing in and out in and out in and out, out of her dripping pussy.

Lake stopped cold.

Lindsey-Smith slapped her.

"You want some mouth you better show me some lesbian pussy." She dragged the tip of her tongue down the clit's legs to the cave, which puckered up and sucked it in and squeezed it before expelling it with coochie juice. "Show me what *you* got before you piss me off."

Lindsey-Smith walked her begging clit across Lake's tongue,

which succumbed and licked her up so fast she thought she had a bee buzzing up her coochie. "Tear it up, Daddy."

Lake's face was slick with pussy toppings when her lover, on the verge of collapse, pushed it away. Lake mounted Lindsey-Smith and spread her lips exposing the clit and pressed hers to it.

"Baby, it's inflamed."

Lake held her in place. "I'm bout to heal that."

"No honey. It's real sensitive." Lake began grinding in a tight little circle keeping the clits engaged.

"They're stuck together now."

"You greedy."

"*I* tell your coochie when to stop comin. Not you." Lindsey-Smith wanted to slap her, take back control but her shit was cooking. They rode in that tight little circle letting friction have its way with them. Nipples to nipples they maxed out.

Somewhere in the songwriter's head she heard an old lesbian lullaby. *Jellybean, jellybean, so firm, so smooth, so obscene. Jellybean, jellybean where you been? Jellybean, jellybean, so obscene. Your pussy fits my face from clit to cave to chin.* Lindsey-Smith slept electric.

Nightmares unplugged repeating Cindy's wishscape alternately with Jason Bank's wishscape in an endless loop that snapped flinging Lindsey-Smith's essence, those pesky neutrons, skyward where they formed a constellation kneeling in prayer sprinkling starlight on the blue planet on a clearing in a woods where seven-year olds wearing school uniforms kicked to death a classmate, a girl wearing a yellow headscarf. From the praying constellation a star that formed its heart fell across earth and disappeared forever into that black hole that gelatinous legs straddled.

35

10:04 pm. Halloween. PCH.

The horizon should have touched the sky where cars leaped off like lemans. And true to itself the closer Dracula got to the horizon the further away it moved.

Scree loosened by the rain forced the cars in front of the Mercedes to swerve. It took flight over the debacle. Deliriously happy squeals from Dracula joined the sound track as the car landed solidly on all fours.

Dracula's driving skills weren't as highly evolved as the Mercedes technology, which illustrated its skills when it snatched away control. As if a switch had been flipped Swan Neck set up ramrod straight, snatched the wheel with a porcelain white hand, brought the car under control, and culminated the event by slumping down in the passenger seat. Her severely elongated neck twisted so that she could see Dracula with the eyes she didn't have.

His laughter roared. "The witch assigned to me against my will gots the benefits. It drives while blind."

"You're blind, too, fool. Don't forget the fuckin facts."

Lightening flashed zigzag across the ink sky exposing several cars considerably ahead of the black Mercedes. The little orange Corvette never looked back, her rear lights running red repeatedly braking in respect for Satan's highway, terror induced by those creatures determined to have her.

Cars pulled aside for the black car. Behind it they closed up like a zipper.

"This is awesome." Dracula gleefully exploded like a true immortal happy with pursuing someone to death. Without warning the Mercedes hydroplaned around a twist in the highway."

"You tryin to kill yourself?"

"What do you mean? I'm dead. Oh, I know. That stuff about sunlight. A stake through my heart. I'm into that shit." He said prideful.

"That's Hollywood, Flash. Your make-up doesn't come off. Like my neck. There are simpler ways to die again. Unless drivin off this mountain is your thing. By the way, the word immortal is over used. Don't get stupid! We're out here to win souls. And she's it. Not us!"

"But I'm dead, asshole."

"Energy never dies. It enters the black hole. That's why we're here. We don't want to go there. Ride that orange to hell."

36

Satan and his human mentor walked upon earth surveying his hordes with his penetrating presence, when it was bloodied with humanity, "Condemnment four. Believe in luck and you believe in me."

His unlucky minions dropped their pants and grabbed their ankles. With his million-headed cock he fucked them inside out until they resembled the plastinated people in a museum display of cadavers. When his cock heads were mangled with putrid muck, his mighty groin cracked the earth somewhere in California.

37

"Come back here, woman." Lake reached for Lindsey-Smith, but she evaded her and landed awkwardly on the oak floor.

Slapping Lake's hand, "You stop. My stuff's jumpin. I shouldn't've been lovin you all night cause I damn near can't move."

Lake slid onto the floor next to Lindsey-Smith. "Before you put the Ace Bandage back on I'll rub some Tiger Balm on you. Hmmm, now that's a fantasy—"

Lindsey-Smith cut her short. "It burns."

Lake dragged her nipples along Lindsey-Smith's shoulder blades. "Let's trade fantasies. What's yours?" She brushed her pubic hairs lightly back and forth across Lindsey-Smith's butt.

Lindsey-Smith submitted, leaning back into Lake, "I've only had two fantasies in my life—" she spat venom, "—torturin the monster who took my sister." She smiled, more inside than out. "And fallin in love telepathically."

"Can't help you with those. C'mon, give me something I can make happen." She kissed her nape.

"Oh, you did that." She stepped away from the inevitable. "Now get back. Don't misunderstand, I like that in you." Lake flashed teeth. "The next time you hold me down I'll slap the shit out of you. You believe me?"

Thrown for a loop Lake could hardly say no. "Yeah."

"Good." She strolled towards the bathroom. "You wouldn't've gotten any more of this," she rubbed her crotch, "if you had said 'no'." She averted her eyes from the wardrobe mirror. The last thing she needed to see was how messed up she looked. "The 7s Killer had to kill Jason for a compellin reason, don't you think? I think he interrupted the prick gettin his freak on. Otherwise, why would the scumbag even be in the woods? I mean." They entered the master bathroom.

Green marble tiles, trees and plants under a skylight brought the outdoors inside.

"I'm way ahead of you. If that's true there should be evidence of the serial's presence. A broken twig. Trampled undergrowth; it was a soggy night. If the tracks match those we found at Cindy Patron's crime site we got ourselves a little somethin somethin. The clincher would be findin evidence of him, or the girl, in a clearin near Banks. Don't you worry bout it. I'm handlin business. My way." Lake bent over the natural stone whirlpool tub and turned it on.

"An eighty-five year-old dyke once told me there's lesbian pussy and then there's regular." As she looked straight up at the bossy woman's red pocketbook Lindsey-Smith smiled at her problem, which she recognized as hopeless, for if a woman showed it to her she had to kiss it. When Lake reached to feel the water's temperature, as the water spilled between her fingers, Lindsey-Smith slipped inside Lake's warm pool. Grabbing a handful of weave, praying it would hold, she pulled Lake's head back forcing her butt to back up and take all the fingers. Lindsey-Smith tapped bottom. "That's what they mean by piano fingers." She whispered, her lips lightly touching Lake's ear.

They lay back, sprawled out and panting in the whirlpool for several minutes.

Lake howled, "Taint nothin like a be'atch havin her stuff worked in the mornin, nasty heifer." Lake cooed.

"Nasty fantasy."

"What do you know bout my fantasies?"

"Did you forget that I read minds?" Lake sat up, inspecting Lindsey-Smith's eyes for a clue to her sincerity. "How else would I know?" She smiled sheepishly, then seeing Lake's expression turn ugly, "Of course I didn't read your mind, Lady Remarkable. I don't have it like that."

Lake spread her legs letting jets of bubbles pop her virgina. "But still. I did imagine how hot it would be if you caught me off guard. Then I feel you all up inside my stuff. I'm just sayin."

"Your fantasy played to my weakness, leave no pussy in distress."

Lake kicked water in Lindsey-Smith's face and dove under water to her.

Lindsey-Smith's eyes rolled back in her head. Like cars on a racetrack girls' faces swooshed by accompanied by a sound track; suzysallylizzycatissayoucan'thaveitit'smine. A hand on her shoulder shaking her now, shaking her eyes open in the real world, "— tissa." She shouted. Under Lake's calming hand her shoulder turned to rattlesnakes driving her out of the tub. Behind her trailed a river.

"Who's *Tissa*, be'atch?" The detective asked disappointed, the warmth sucked out of her voice.

"Catissa."

"You said *Tissa*.... *Catissa*? Wait. Just wait damnit!" Lindsey-Smith thought Lake looked like she was going to be sick. "Can't be that many girls named Catissa. What made you say that name?"

Lindsey-Smith's toes curled up against the marble floor's chill. She flipped a switch turning on the heater embedded in the floor. "What's wrong, Lake?"

"I haven't told you about Catissa Barnes because we're waitin to confirm the ID. We think that's Angel Doe's name, the vic you saw Halloween. Where'd you get the name Catissa from?"

"The wishscape." She wiped off Lake's back with a thick white towel enjoying the contrast with Lake's bronze skin. "You used your cop's voice." The admonishing tone sullied the air between the two women, an outcome she hadn't considered before she whined.

"We don't have enough time for me to change my ways. It's disingenuous for either of us to expect it." She snatched the towel and began toweling Lindsey-Smith. "Talk to me, honey."

A minute passed.

"It sounds like gibberish cause he's thinkin thoughts. The faces are smears. But not those eyes. I see em. I see em real good. All the little girls, their eyes askin me to help them. 'Suzy Sally Betsey Lizzy Cindy Catissa give it back to me you can't have it.'" She stopped having hit the wall. "There's more. I hear it. But it's gibberishy. You look sick."

"We have possibly two victims who fit two of those names, Cindy and Catissa. Suzy, Sally, Betsey aren't victims."

"Only thing that makes sense."

"Many things could make sense." Lake wrapped a dry towel around her hair and made her exit.

Lindsey-Smith straggled out of the bathroom, crossed the expansive bedroom to a nightstand where she grabbed a yellow note pad and pencil from a drawer and began writing down the names before they hid themselves. "Granted you don't have any dead girls with those names. Up there in his head where it counts, he's got em. If he thinks they're dead then they're dead. Do you think, girlfriend? The fact that you don't know about them attests to how little you cops know."

Lake pulled jeans over raw pussy as she prepared for the walk of shame, which an area of Lindsey-Smith's brain imagined Lake walking to the soaring theme music of the TV series *Stargate_Atlantis*. She felt closer to her, like she could be herself without complaint. She took a chance.

"Here's what I know. I can match one set of eyes up with a name—Cindy. He calls up their names and their faces. I see the world die in those girls' eyes whose names you don't know. I've got their eyes in death lookin back at me. Oh they're dead all right."

"Here's what I know. He's been at it a long time because he never makes a mistake. Practice makes perfect. Nowhere but nowhere is there a record of any crimes remotely similar to ours. Every database, includin Interpol, has been checked more than once. So if there are victims out there they don't fit the present profile, which means he changed. A smart serial does."

"I don't think he changed what you called the target age."

"You know this how?"

"I saw their faces, d'aaamn, Lake. Not for long. But I saw them. They looked seven to me. This reminds me I need the

names of all the murdered girls. The ones you know about."
She held out the pad.

Lake plucked her BlackBerry from a nightstand and punched
several buttons before calling up photos of victims. She passed
the phone to Lindsey-Smith, "Have a go at em. Maybe we'll
luck out and you'll recognize somebody."

Lindsey-Smith tightened her towel around her chest as if
she needed it for support as she sidled over to the front of the
room remembering clearly for the first time a woods where
dormant grass, evergreen trees, bushes plump with red berries,
tree trunks, Cindy's jet black hair, everything was a ghostly
white on white, even the shadows in that world of light that no
human eye could see.

She gingerly lowered her stiff body onto the cushioned
window seat.

Outside her fourth story bedroom double windows, each
a massive four by five feet, the sun rose in the east by design.
She watched it peek boldly over treetops and her neighbor's
roof resisting the urge to open the window and inhale the day,
as was her habit before her ribs became an issue. Without the
benefit of fresh air she refocused on the photos. But first she
checked over her shoulder. The two-headed shadow had her
jumpy like that.

Unable to detach herself from the photos she welcomed
Lake's rescue.

"You recognize her."

Lindsey-Smith nodded. "The eyes...." She let her voice trail
as she passed the phone.

"Number three, Leslie Dawson. You said zip bout him sayin
her name."

"Leslie. Les-lie. Lesss-lie."

"We found her a month after he killed her. Took her mother,
or whatever you wanna call that thing, two weeks to report her
missin. Said she had nine too many kids to miss one."

"What's in a name? Listen to this. Louise Elizabeth Leslie
Cassandra Sarah Cybil Lucinda Sunny Cecelia Missy Felecia.
Felecia? Felecia doesn't fit the pattern. Can you hear it?"

"Our computer team couldn't find any patterns."

"Maybe if they said the names out loud they would've heard all those sibilants."

"Speak English."

"Sibilants. Their names all have *S* sounds except Felecia. That pretty much fucks my theory."

"Maybe not. The mother pronounced it different. If she protected that little girl half as much as she protected the pronunciation of her name that baby would be alive."

"How'd she pronounce it, please?"

"I don't remember. There's an apostrophe after...between the *e* and *c*."

"Fele'cia. Fele—see-a. It fits. You need to be less careless with the English language."

"Humph. Aint that nothin? Picks his victims by the sound of their names. We missed it."

"Sicko is obsessed with the snaky sound. On the video Cindy's mother said the prick liked the sound of Cindy's name."

"You did good, honey." She hit several buttons on her cell and set out pacing the big room. "West, listen up." She explained the sibilants. "Put cadet teams on schools in every crack target area. Pass out flyers. Get em in the assembly halls. And ID as many girls as they can with sibilants in their names with known addicted mothers. He's bout to get thrown off his game." She leaned into the phone as if privatizing the conversation. "You take care of that thing we talked bout? Check it out, the Fibbers are listenin so forget bout tellin me how much you love me." She pocketed the phone. In front of the wardrobe mirror where she strapped on her .9mm she checked out her lover's reflection. "I'm gonna write you a note to remind you to buy a couple of cells. Til then just watch what you say when you call me. I don't trust that concussion of yours. The Fibbers're lookin to pick up the next call from our tipster when he calls me. Only you and I know that aint gonna happen. Let's keep it that way." She slid a .22 into an ankle holster. "Justin Banks anyone?"

38

A brass key turned in the Schlage Lock. With a click the dead bolt released.

"Yesterday almost took me with her." Lindsey-Smith shared as Lake turned the doorknob to the late Justin Banks' studio. "When I write days don't end. They run together like frayed thread with lots of knots and snarls." She explained.

"Shush!" The door swung open into a vintage studio apartment stacked wall-to-wall with moving boxes.

"Can't help it. I'm nervous. I never broke into a place before in my life. Okay?"

Lake drew her gun. Jangling keys, "Not breakin in when you have these." She slid inside. "Chicago police. Lieutenant Lake. Chicago PD. Anyone here?" She announced then turned on the lights with a wall switch. Lindsey-Smith noticed the drapes were drawn tight. "Stay here." When Lake had vetted the micro-space she quietly closed the door as she holstered her weapon. "Banks is the only one who's supposed to live here, but you never know."

"You went back to Possum Woods. Thank you."

"Not me personally. We cops have our ways, too."

Lindsey-Smith came up short as she entered the room. She was an invader and an invisible hand held her back demanding she recognize. "I get this feelin that Justin was a very private man. Secretive even." She opened a box and removed a stack of sheet music. "Opera. You go, boy." She tickled the keys on the studio piano that dominated the room. "Tsk. It's always the good ones they kill." She ran a scale. "It's in tune." She sang *"If I lose, if I lose you, I've lost tomorrow—All my beginnings and all my todays. You're the bursting flowers and the shinning sea."*

Lake tore open another box, rifled through it and announced, "All operas." She withdrew an eight by five black picture frame. "A masters in voice. Brotha was heavy." She wiped a smudge from the glass and returned it to the box.

"His mom must be goin nuts." Suddenly, she missed the weight of her gun, but not the idea of being busted for killing scum. Her nose wrinkled. "Those symbols make sense now, if I think bout them from Jason the musician's perspective." Lake watched over her shoulder as she pointed to a treble clef on a piece of music. "What if that backwards *S* means treble clef? It's the key, stupid. The key to his code." She wrote it out. *: A # : SOL* "The colon's a repeat sign, meanin do it again. He uses it twice I think to emphasize what's important. The *A* is," she played *A* above middle *C* on the piano, "probably high for a man. That pound sign in music means sharp. So it would be," she played *A*-sharp. "Those letters *SOL* I think is the unfinished word *solo*. Because *sun* in Spanish makes no sense next to these other symbols. For whatever reason he didn't finish the word. Maybe he got distracted. He was runnin for his life? Solo means one. What do you think? Your killer works alone."

"I don't know what you just said. Do you?"

"What, my face gives me away? Jason studied voice. In one of these boxes there's gotta be a CD of him singin. Damn. The chance of a life time now lays in boxes of soon to be trash."

"Sounds like you're talkin bout yourself."

"Hope not." She played a phrase from one of her songs. "I would've loved to hear him sing something of mine. Smack me." She slapped her face. "What would he notice about the killer? The voice. Poor soul heard his killer talkin. This is an unusually high male voice he's describin. The pervert has a voice higher than most women's. Uglyyy. I'd know that voice anywhere. He speaks in the key of *A*-sharp"

"Then I say we leave here ASAP so my tone deaf ass can put out an APB on all men who sound like a woman."

"Jason couldn't possibly know that the detective investigatin his death would be tone deaf."

"It's just that this information doesn't get us any closer to stoppin the killer." Lake opened the door. "Any way, anticipation works. In fact, I favor that method. Get there before the serial does and we win. Nice. The anticipation part, it never happens. Cops come after the fact. Before the fact, you're on your own."

"So people should carry guns."

"That's a leap."

"So's a dog name Symbol."

39

The neat middleclass street on which Jason Banks once lived belied his ugly murder with its proud homes and manicured lawns, too green for the drought. She fingered the knot on her forehead. Naughty people. No respect for the rest of Chicago who let their grass die to save water for the trees. It wasn't such a pretty street when she looked at it like that.

Lake ended her call and bounded down the steps to the sidewalk where Lindsey-Smith waited noting that the woman appeared positively enraged in a controlled sista way, just shy of the hands on the hips. Lake's claws came out.

"Did you think they wouldn't notice the eight hundred pound gun in the room?"

"Uh oh. I've got a license." Taking her wallet out she handed it to Lake who slapped it aside.

"How dare you? I can't believe you kept that from me." She grabbed her head.

"I didn't have the time or opportunity to go through it. And we still don't have the luxury."

"You're makin me crazy. You said nothin to me, a go'damn po-lice officer, bout packin a gun. That's just plain fucked up. And I know you know better. If not we can't have a conversation."

"You want me to say I was wrong? You know I was wrong. Do you think I don't know I fucked up? I had a good reason at the time. All ego and a little bit of substance. I was just out to get the pussy. Beyond that nothin. You know what you got down there. You saw how it was doin me. So don't play like you don't. I don't share with people who plan on stayin a hot minute in my life. There wouldn't be any thing left of me if I did." She glanced up and down the street noting light traffic and three pedestrians who should've been in school.

"Who did you bribe to get your firearm license?"

"Fuck you, Lake."

"You did that already." Moving towards the Crown Victoria parked at the curb Lindsey-Smith felt a pull from the red brick Victorian building they had just vacated. She turned back. "Now where you goin? You're messin with my karma." She pointed to Jason's windows where the drapes remained pulled against the day's light. "You should've told me, heifer."

"Nothin's gonna get in the way of what I have to do. I'll make mistakes. Bite me. In the end I fuckin rock his cycle in the universe. Nobody else. Me. It's all on me. Not you." She walked up the steps. "I need to go back in. Something's there and I just missed it. Jason wouldn't be in the wishscape if he was meaningless."

"Why such a big gun, Lindsey?" She slammed the car door shut and came around the front of the car.

She held up her hands, "Huge hands."

"This isn't about sex."

Lake stalked across the grass and got in her face. "One of those men who tried to beat me to death, I blew his stupid head off."

"You didn't." Incredulity sapped her anger.

"I was there. Little girls don't have the time for me to confess and go through the system."

"Cindy Patron and a woman in Wicker Park, who got hydrochloric acid tossed in her face, were the only two fatalities in Chicago Halloween and the day after."

The wisher could feel the old man's hands all over it. Her head throbbed. No Icabod Crane, no dog named Symbol, no tavern, just bruises and cuts all over her body.

"Can you shoot?"

She felt Lake tucking her passion back inside where she kept it safe from casual relationships. She couldn't blame her. But this wasn't about her. Stay on point, Lindsey-Smith.

"Can you shoot?"

"Every Thursday at a burbie shootin range I shoot the eye out of a newt. Okay, maybe not. You openin this door anytime soon?"

Lake grabbed her by the elbow. "This serial is a professional killer in case you didn't notice. And in case you don't know what that means he won't hesitate to kill you."

"Then we have that in common. Open the door."

"You won't see him before he sees you."

"I don't plan on losin." She glanced up at the Jason's red brick building admiring its slender aristocratic silhouette between chunky gray stone buildings, sort of like Lena Horne in a little black dress standing between two General Powells. "Just so you know, I care what one hell of a woman thinks."

It worked; Lake backed off. She checked her Timex. "We've got an appointment with Brenda Patron. With an addict time is everything. Two minutes." She reached into her leather coat pocket and extracted the keys, "Two minutes. I mean it." She threatened.

Lindsey-Smith's eyes were drawn to Jason's window where the drapes moved. "Did you see that?" Lake following her eyes looked up seeing nothing she proceeded to put the key in the lock. "Look, something moved those drapes."

"The wind. Stop everything. The windows are closed."

"Yeah." The Victorian leaned, it turrets sagging like size 'EE' tits towards her. Goosebumps crawled on her scalp as she instinctively shuffled backwards towards the sidewalk. "RUN!" Her uncool turned to terror. She grabbed Lake's arm. She resisted. Lindsey-Smith shoved her. "Look!"

The sound of a freight train rumbling down the tracks chased then down the middle of the street. When the noise ceased they stopped. Out of breath they dared to look back. Red bricks bounced just shy of their feet.

"That's a clue you weren't meant to have." Lake said catching her breathe.

Lindsey-Smith clutched the ribcage that wouldn't let her catch her breath. "Hope nobody was home."

"The other two floors are empty. Can't even see my car.

D'aaamn" Lake called for help as the street suddenly swarmed with the curious and helpful snapping pictures of the collapsed Victorian and calling 9-1-1. Car alarms screamed piercing the buzz of excited voices. The songwriter in Lindsey-Smith heard an orchestra hip-hopping in hell all boom and shrieks.

"Maybe there was no clue in there. If those drapes hadn't moved when they did.... How did they move?"

"Don't care. They stopped us from being buried under a ton of bricks."

"We were warned."

The bewildered crowd navigated towards them. Lake, seeing them, raised her badge and announced that she was a cop.

"If I were a man you'd lay a fat kiss on me right here for saving your butt."

Lake untucked her passion and kissed her ending with a little tongue. Phone cameras snapped away.

"You know, every woman I get with someway somehow I end up doin a rescue. When she gets on her feet she throws me away like a pair of old crutches. I thought you were different. I thought you'd rescue me."

Taken aback Lake stormed, "Didn't see that comin."

"I didn't mean that the way it came out."

"Hope not." She sounded unsure to Lindsey-Smith.

"Truth be told, something not of this world saved us."

"You mean the devil saved us." She seethed.

"To keep us in the game." Everything in her world turned white on white.

40

The partially blocked sunlight shone its remnants on Brenda Patron's handless corpse lying between DUMPSTERS lined up against the common brick wall of a seedy apartment building.

Both ends of the alley were V-D off with blue and whites, their rack lights seriously swirling over Brenda whose cracked lips pulled back in a grimace that mimicked the gapping ear-to-ear slash from which her life poured down the alley's gutter past a crushed box of cornflakes into a sewer.

Doctor Perez shifted her weight, wearing latex gloves she gestured, demonstrating the words she explained. "Usually, the perp pulls the head back and slashes upward toward himself." She stood her head level with Lake's shoulders. "That method gets the blood all over him. Your killer pressed her head forward. Cut in a downward stroke." She let that sink in.

"Humph." Lake stepped up. "That method allowed him to control the blood spray. He walked out of here without a drop of blood on him."

"Probably. Heard you and your hot girlfriend brought down the house, or should I say building?" The M.E. teased.

"We got it like that."

A uniform uttered uncomfortably, "Nobody saw nothin, Lieu. You believe that?"

From some of the windows overlooking the alley peered faces that had witnessed violent death before. Lake scanned them. Not one pulled their wide-eyed child away from the windows. A cat scampered down the alley and disappeared under a dilapidated wood fence. Agitated dogs barked.

"She didn't deserve this, Doc."

"Nobody does." The doctor added altruistically, like a true Ann Rand lover.

"Some people do." Lake said matter-factually. "Some people do." The finality of her somber tone made the doctor do a double take.

From a window directly above them a woman's voice shouted obscenities. A shoe followed hitting the uniform in the back. He cursed.

"We can thank Connors for losin the best witness we've ever had. The perp bailed her out so he could silence her. I'd say he was worried about what she might remember. He won't be leavin any more witnesses. Aint that right, Brenda?"

Two homicide detectives huddled around West who pulled at his droopy slacks. "Lieutenant, Detective Spencer's all over the bail bondsman like lady diarrhea. Knows him personal. Says an ol black woman paid with crisp twenties printed in—"

Lake finished his sentence. "Nineteen eighty-seven in sequential order."

"Twenty years back when he socked it away he didn't think we'd be able to follow da money. He means them twenties to be his signature. Let us know he's been there. That's why he socked it away. Our boy's been plannin on this a spell." His Alabama drawl took so long to finish Lake forgot what he was talking about.

"Okay with that, West."

West peeled away from the huddle pointing up where charcoal clouds intermittently blocked out the sun. "Sho do look like rain, Lieu."

A dark blue unmarked skidded to a stop behind the yellow tape attracting attention. Connors emerged barking commands as he swaggered down the alley. "I want everything handled by the book. No fuck-ups people." He aimed the last statement at Lake who sneered in reply. "Nothin goes wrong. Make sure that building doesn't fall on the body, Lake."

Crime scene technicians and West, who had turned their efforts to beating the rain, didn't hear Connors but the distant rolling thunder huffing and puffing in the belly of ever darkening clouds. It scalded Connors' Bonaparte ego that nobody bothered to answer him. He stood around like a stick with nothing to stir. The man was set to have a serial collar on his arrest record. He couldn't have written a better script. Furthermore, he could count on the task force doing everything within their skills to stop the sociopath. Certainly they didn't want him to get the credit, but that wouldn't slow them down. They all hated people who hurt children. They respected that he was one of them in that regard, an elite few dedicated to doing something about it.

Halfway out of the alley Lake caught up with Connors who put a hand on a hip. "What?"

"It's your fault she's dead. How's that feelin right bout now?"

"Insubordination." He snapped.

"She's dead, fool. Insubordinate that!" She pointed behind her at Patron's body.

"There's no hard evidence connectin that ho's death to our case. None."

"You know this how because you need to tell that to the media?" She smirked at the news vans parking next to his car. "They want to know. Shall we talk to em?"

A teapot on the boil, Connors spilled over, "We won't do this now. FYI. The super's callin a news conference." He stomped off ignoring the pleas of the Media.

West knelt at Patron's side. Lake joined him. "This killer's bold as shit on new snow."

"He's full blown. Smart. Wealthy. A chameleon. He cut off her hands because she outfoxed him. She must've scratched him." Shoving West back, away from Patron's legs, she cocked her head to get a better angle. "Is that smeared blood, Doc? Right there between her thighs." She and West made room for Doctor Perez.

"Might be." The doctor murmured examining the smudges. "Blood there makes no sense."

Lake looked closer. "Check it for DNA. I think I just got a new respect for Patron, you know what I mean?"

"We'll check all the blood stains for DNA." She cleared her throat. "I'm sorry about Chief Boggs. She was a great detective. Phenomenal. I heard you two were close."

Lake hurried away from the sympathy. "Well, now we've got Connors. You're lookin at the result on the ground there."

The M.E. lowered her voice. "He's got his own problems I heard from a very reliable source."

"Yeah? Exactly what did you hear, girlfriend?"

"The universe is full of quarks."

"We go back fifteen years, Rachael and I."

"Think about all those random quarks."

41

Lindsey-Smith entered her closet-sized music studio located in the basement of her studio. A red robin perched on the windowsill asked her how it came to be there at night, and then flew to the cyclone fence that surrounded her backyard and perched next to a female, its belly rustic red like blood smudges. But she couldn't see those colors that she knew must be there.

The lovers took flight with the falling of the first raindrops. "Cowards."

She had grieved at the news of Brenda Patron's death. If nothing else she had big hopes the woman might trigger more memories. Those hopes died with Patron, so said the beat-up reflection in the windowpane super-imposed on the white-flocked world outside. Inside, plenty of the same. The riotous colors of her walls had faded into shades of white-on-white. She rubbed her eyes. She was white. That meant Lake was white. Black people were white. What would they do if they knew? Would a whole bunch of peeps line up? Would there be any blacks left in America?

As she passed the piano she plunked high A-sharp.

She ran angry arpeggios up and down the piano as fast as her fingers allowed until she was exhausted, until her fingers stiffened, until her butt ached. Until she felt better. And then worst. Like the cops she too was stuck waiting for the killer's next move. Suddenly, as if the piano had insulted her, she scooted away from it. "Only a fool waits for death."

Neatly arranged on her desk, books: *Broadway Musicals*, *Annie Leibovitz*, *I Dream A World*, *Asterix and the Black Gold*, and *True Crimes*; an OTT-LITE, a yellow legal pad on which lay a black ZEBRA pen. Sheet music overflowed from in and out baskets. Unopened bills lay on the floor where she dropped them the day after the gates of hell opened up and swallowed her life.

The books were gifts from women she loved. The iconic photograph of John Lennon and Yoko Ono on a cover flipped on the reminiscent switch calling forth the woman who gave her the book and her gentle eye for art. She removed the Leibovitz from between its zebra bookends. *True Crimes* fell to the floor open.

"Stay there." No way was she bending over to pick up a book. That was just like Caroline, expecting Lindsey-Smith to bend over backwards till it hurt to please her, yet unable to please herself; she was dark that way with lips that could suck the bumper off a Hummer.

A steady downpour turned on like a shower head at full blast cleaning the city, sloshing off its big shoulders—too much, too fast—sending the home owner to check her sump pump happy her studio was raised several feet off the floor. A flood would ruin her financially, not to mention professionally. She couldn't afford to rent an outside studio.

And she definitely couldn't afford to lose the income on studio rental.

She opened the back door leading from the basement to the backyard. It rained. She inhaled. The sun had escaped the day leaving behind a dirty sheet reminiscent of Catissa's rotted white dress. Jagged lightening bolted east ripping apart the flat bottom clouds. She counted; "Elephant one elephant two—" Thunder struck something. Its laughter rumbled around in the belly of the clouds spilling its guts in buckets. Lightening ripped the sheet to shreds. A string of skylights embedded in the shreds flickered on and off like Christmas lights. She closed her eyes tight against the rain smelling a sweet cloying chemical. Prickles rose all over her body. The world around her dissolved. The world beyond it peeled back in layers exposing her stupidity. It was happening to her again. The sky roared girls' names. Enraged, the killer's fingers tingled as they readied themselves for murder. His soul roiled. Her eyes opened to the horror she knew she would see through his eyes in his white on white concave world.

One fuckin wish the old fart said. Now she saw the trick or treats possibilities, the same wish over and over every time he attacked a girl until she stopped him. White watch face. White crown. Nine fifty two. GPS coordinates. Girl's wild white eyes that seemed to look right at her. They pleaded for help, instantly disappointment and accusations followed. In them Lindsey-Smith saw herself become what she hated most, someone who hurt children. Names came faster faster. Faster.

She stood ankle deep in water her hands splayed out in front of her. She howled at the cunty sky that dared piss in her mouth. The horny straight woman next door, bare breasted, stared out the window at her. The rain sizzled. Lindsey-Smith slammed the door.

A dragon tail shaped lightening bolt sketched Satan's profile across the red and blue sky.

She dragged her sopping wet butt into the office. On the floor, *True Crimes* lay opened to a page with Jeffrey Dahmer's photo. His eyes stuttered her steps; one degree of separation came to mind as she hesitated to pick up the phone. Lake's warning about the FBI listening in on her cell reverberated in her head. Thank God she remembered. The call had to be made from an untraceable phone. Unfortunately, when The Chief was shot, they forgot all about the throwaways. With a perfect storm in her soul she blew out the house, a desperate umbrellaless woman with the name Zoë on her tongue, and terrorized white eyes in her heart, what was left of it.

42

It was eight o'clock in the morning and JP steamed behind his desk in his corner office. He slammed his fist on the old oak desk. The pencils jumped and rolled to the floor. The man had been up all night, not that that bothered him for he could pull an all-nighter with the best of them. But that hadn't been on his agenda. The whole thing had forced him to rearrange his life. Cunts had fucked his life up. Put his shit on fast track. How the fuck dare they?

From his listening nook he heard the investigators say the dyke detective received the tip about the murder of a child named Zoë from an anonymous tip. The caller had given the precise location of the body.

That was good. He realized that the Lieutenant didn't want her colleagues to know that she was dabbling in the supernatural. "Good for me." Until that Lindsey-Smith cunt came alone the cops had nothing. Fifteen minutes after he did it the cops jumped on it, bearing down on his picnic spot with Zoë. He barely got away.

How the bitch found the exact location evaded him. That shit didn't matter though. "How is for nerds, the profilers." What mattered was he didn't know how much she knew or how close she was to knowing maybe his damn address. He looked around the office that had, after nineteen years, become foreign to him in the last year when his new boss, an old enemy, took over the office, when it turned deadly for seven-year old girls.

And they could thank Prince, JP's boss, for it.

He put his head down on the desk. A jade green translucent jar packed with a bouquet of bright colored lollipops wrapped in cellophane graced the beat-up desk in the position where most people displayed the obligatory framed family photograph of homely spouses and children. A bronze nameplate read: JOAQUIN PRIEST.

With his back to the closed door of his cramped office JP's stubby fingers delicately danced clicking keys on a keyboard. He felt a breeze at his back. His fingers stopped and hung above the keyboard. Languidly, he turned to face Prince, the man that dared threaten his pension, the reason he killed to maintain control of his drives. Drives that Prince had set prematurely in motion.

To Stanford Prince, a sloped-shoulder well-dressed giant, Priest deserved all the ugly the world had to offer. Fifteen years ago he lost an important promotion because Priest eliminated the job in a department re-make. It took five years to make-up for that lost ground. The first day on his new job it angered him that JP smugly didn't recall the event.

Both men smiled falsely into the other's face.

Prince fished a lollipop from the jar and examined it with a scowl. "Do you have to make my jaw line look like Jay Leno's?" He impaled the lollipop in his pinstripe lapel. "You're creepy, Priest. But you make awesome suckers." He flashed his best Machiavellian smile. "Why don't you quit? You don't need the money. That's okay. Stay, my little baby. I'm going to rock your cradle. You know it's comin down the pike, don't you. I'm callin in all my favors. I know where all the important pussies and dicks meet. People prefer I stay quiet and happy." He laughed straightening his polka dot tie, and then sauntered to the door, and out.

JP shot to his feet. "Die a creepy death." He blew a kiss in Prince's direction.

As of today he had worked nineteen years, six months and six days to earn his retirement, his poppy's dream that he promised on his deathbed to fulfill. It was all he had of his father's. The element magnetized him so completely he didn't stray into his natural predilection, killing girls. In fact, he found an alternative death to tide him over until he reached his twenty years and freedom to do his thing. He closed the door gently. "My pension, Prince. Mine. It's Mine you can't have it."

JP, lost in revelry, was interrupted by a woman living life as the Pillsbury Dough Girl who entered announcing, "Knock knock!" Her pale blue eyes latched onto the green jar and hung out among the pretty candy. The puffy woman talked as if a longtime friendship existed between them, pissing off JP because the office believed it. "Your caricature lollipops are great. Guess you know that." She extracted a lollipop and admired its cherry red lips and blueberry eyes. "This is Irma's. Ohhh, I wish you'd do me. Oh, I didn't mean it like that." He pierced her chest with his unblinking eyes.

She must have said goodbye because when JP noticed she was gone. The cell on his hip buzzed. He read the caller ID. "That works." He answered. Tapping out a rhythm on his desk with the eraser head of a mechanical pencil, his eyebrows, although shaved, raised in disbelief.

"No known psychic phenomenon. No such thing? Great! I paid you to tell me you don't know." He closed the clamshell phone.

A vise tightened around his head. That bad feeling swam down through his blood stream. "She just stepped into my brain." He conceded. Not knowing what had been stole while the woman held residence inside his mind created urgent solutions: he could shoot her dead when she stepped out of her front door; he could run her over when she crossed the street; he could happily cut her throat. "Get up and do it. Just do it, fool. Get caught, why don't you, asshole." There was something to be said for spontaneity. Had he done them when the urge struck…he quickly dismissed second guessing himself.

At Strogers ER he could've had two for one. But that was not the ending he wrote having the police on his tail as a cop killer. Nope. Every cop in the world would want a piece of his ass.

From his briefcase he removed a sheet of paper with a list of names. With a stab of his forefinger he chose one, circling it with a red marker until it bled. It seemed a far better idea to find a way to destroy Lindsey-Smith before she did him in with the brain invasions. Two could play mind games. Two could win if one of them was dead.

He rubbed his left wrist trying to remember where he put the wristband GPS. It hit him; that had to be how the cops knew precisely where to find the bodies so soon after he left them.

"No way."

Imagination being what it was, intensely personal, his had failed to imagine anyone accessing his brain, but he accepted it as fact. Similarly, he accepted eyes that could see through his. In fact, he blessed the concept because it put a check in his winning column.

43

Lindsey-Smith sat on the edge of the seat then slid her body into it. The restaurant smells assailed her nose. Her stomach growled at the plate of bacon and eggs that the waitress sat in front of Lake who immediately began inhaling it. "Aren't you hungry, baby?" Lake asked her with a full mouth.

"No."

"When was the last time you ate?" She crumbled a slice of bacon on her eggs. "Hmm hmmm. I've always been partial to pancake houses." She forked in raspberry pancakes dripping with raspberry syrup and raspberry butter. "You need to eat, lady." She shook her head. "Fine. Starve." She drained the cup and signaled the waitress with the empty cup.

Her phone sang. "Lindsey-Smith! Hey, Rita." She switched ears. "I'm good. The surgery went great. No, the patient didn't die. Sorry I didn't check back in with you." After a chatty moment she said her good-byes. "Later, angel."

Lake stopped eating. "Who's Rita?" Her eyes bore into her lover's.

"She's a friend with benefits." She let that hang out there. "She dates only doctors. So if you want a lesbian doctor, go see Rita." She smiled at the unintentional double entendre. The waitress sat a pot of coffee on the table. After a moment she poured a cup. "The last time I drank coffee was in New Orleans visitin Rita, two days before Hurricane Katrina. I just had to have some Jamaican Blue Mountain. My stomach got so queasy...."

"So why're you drinkin it, silly?"

"It could help caffeine and all that."

"Help what?"

She looked around to see who might be listening. "You know." She leaned across the table and whispered. "I've gotta have something to stop me from goin under when he attacks. I'm no good paralyzed."

"Somehow I don't think caffeine will do it. Besides, if you don't go under maybe you don't get in his head. Did you think of that?" Lindsey-Smith pushed the cup aside. "Yeah, that's what I thought." She gobbled down the pancakes. "You know I never gain an ounce?"

"Don't brag. You aint middle-age, yet." She didn't want to change the subject until Lake had at least a minute to enjoy the taste of her food.

"That was a bad scene. He killed the mother. Changed his MO after Patron. From here on out he'll kill the mothers."

"I was tryin not to bring it up while you're eatin."

"Why? Oh. Nothin bothers my stomach."

"I see. Didn't realize you ate so much."

"I'm a glutton. You should know that by now."

"Guess I do."

"You should. It's important to me that my women know me. That way there can be no bad surprises like wakin up and findin me sittin on your face." She downed a half of glass of milk. "Got three fuckin hours of sleep last night. You see these bags?" She pointed to the dark bags under her eyes. "I've got bags piggybackin bags."

"The raccoon effect is kinda interestin." Lake just said *my women*. The concept made her head swim. Was she Lake's woman? Better leave that alone. If she asked for elaboration she could find herself in one of those discussions that always end with false feelings expressed, those heat of the moment feelings.

"I figure our racoon eyes complement each other. Lindsey, I really wanna thank you again. We found chloroform traces on the last two girls thanks to their remains bein discovered early. Chloroform doesn't stick around long. That's why we didn't know until now."

Lindsey-Smith sniffed. "How's chloroform smell?"

"Mmmm. Sweet, like a saccharine sweet chemical and the doctor's office. I know that look. You smelled it on the vics didn't you? You did. You just blinked twice. Whew. We're tryin to find out where he got the stuff. But that's a long shot. Think winnin the lottery. The shit's not that hard to get over the Internet." She decimated the stack of six pancakes without loosing a drop of syrup yet managed to look sexy. "I think he chose Chicagoland because we've got hectares of forest preserves and woods. He knows we can't cover one thousandth of them. I mean, think bout it. He's been plannin this for twenty years. You keep blinkin."

"Do something. Distract him. Make him redirect his plans."

"Not smart. We don't want this bastard escalatin."

"Escalatin? Can he escalate more than he has? I'm sayin what do you call what he's doin now, cruisin?"

"My job is to protect the least of us."

"Can we blow this pop stand?" The smell of frying bacon turned her stomach shades of blue.

"Hmmm. I love the smell of bacon and coffee in the mornin. Hint hint." She dug out her wallet exposing the gun on her hip.

"How many guns do you carry?"

"Three."

"Thought you guys only carried two." She blinked repeatedly. It didn't help. Lake remained a white woman. But those white eyes halted the blinking.

"I hate bein predictable. Don't you?" She laid cash on the table. "You can get your gun back this mornin. They did note that it's been fired. And nobody reported a man killed on the Westside Halloween night. We'd know that by now. The legless man, huh? This is so far out there I wonder bout me, ya know. If I had enough time to think bout it I'd probably snap." She adjusted her bra. "You have a funny look in your eyes. Stop lyin to me bout it." And she hit the floor heading for the door.

The anger on which Lake rode out whipped around and slapped Lindsey-Smith across her sore cheek. She couldn't believe the sense of abandonment she felt and the guilt.

The shadow slipped through the glass in the door and joined her.

Abandonment aside, if she had a plan, and she didn't, she wouldn't tell Lake. She couldn't tolerate being questioned every step of the way. Or maybe that was good. It forced her to think. Thinking was good.

For a moment she considered that she might be paranoid. Or hypersensitive. That long walk to the exit lasted an hour, each step heavier than the next as a piece of a plan unfolded. He wouldn't like it a bit if his little ritual was made public. And his collection of names, nobody knows about three of those girls. Too bad Lake couldn't use the information without exposing herself to ridicule and possible dismissal.

She asked the devil, "Every little slight offends you, doesn't it?" The waitress thinking she was talking to her twirled around and got the hell away.

An explosion rocked Lindsey-Smith's world. They had a friend in common: technology.

44

"What time's the news conference?" Lake, talking on her cell phone, asked. "My day just keeps gettin shittier." Lindsey-Smith exited the restaurant as a car sped by doing sixty with speakers banging out hip-hop. "If I wasn't on this case I'd give her ass a big ol ticket." Lake railed stomping. D'aamn. Can you believe that? Don't just shrug it off, Lindsey. She had to be doin sixty. Look at her. She blew the stop sign."

Lindsey-Smith was half way down the block headed for her parent's green Rover when Lake drove up in a Crown Victoria and honked. "You just walked away from me. Okay. Okay. I'm a bitch. I warned you it was my middle name. Speakin strictly from love your ass needs to toughen up. But who am I to say?" She burned rubber.

"Whew!" A brotha said as he walked by. "She hot at you!" He shook his head and pimped walked on down the street.

Lake had gotten to her she conceded. The gas tank got to her next. After exiting the gas station the Rover headed to Geek's Café. The plan was simple. Every Geek's Café in America was the same. She'd been in one in at least thirty-six states during her touring days with her old band, back when she thought she could sing. She could count on getting what she needed there—anonymity. And a teenager with an ATM card looking for cold cash to help PC dummies, which she was not. However, she was traceable. Still was, although traceable back to a teen that would not bother to look at her twice.

Lindsey-Smith had the killer to thank for the idea. That moment when she realized the idea came from him it had rocked her world. If he could turn technology against the cops, she could turn it against him. As she pulled into a Geek's Café parking lot a black van jumped out in front of her and slammed on its breaks. She stomped the Rover's brake pedal. The van's door flew open. The shadow laid its flat heads in her lap.

45

10:05 p.m. Halloween. PCH.

Raging rain whipped the winding California road to the sky like the beast it was; whipped the orange Corvette until with brakes screaming pathetically, it challenged a concrete embankment and lost. Jass's sixteen-year-old DD breasts slammed into the steering wheel, simultaneously, the black Mercedes center punched the Corvette's driver side. The penetration complete, the cars now one, appeared like twisted orange and black goblins reaching O-highs in randy passion.

Jass's fading thoughts admonished you're going to die.

Unconsciousness obliterated all next thoughts.

The Corvette and Mercedes rocked deadly on an outcropping to a score composed by chaos; dust churned up by their confrontation sprinkled them with morbid finality.

Below roaring waves crashed against rocks and withdrew in a repetitive melodramatic entreat: Come join my wet depths. At least that was Jass's take on it when she briefly regained consciousness and sang those words through a mouthful of windshield.

46

"Nobody knows the trouble they've seen." Satan laughed gently. Then boomed, "Condemnment five." Amused with himself, he snarled his toothy grin.

The human mentor sensed his vulnerability and cringed remembering until that morning he lived and no one ever noticed he was alive. He had had a job that nobody wanted, not even him. He had lain in a coffin and nobody noticed he was in it. He wanted desperately to understand the fifth condemnment to achieve it, but dared not ask.

47

The police station isn't where Lindsey-Smith thought she would be beginning the meat of her day, which is what she considered mid-morning. The day she had in mind didn't cuff her to an S and M evidence recovery technician with an identical twin in every way. She learned from a gossip-girl friend that they liked to work the dykes' nerves. Apparently, there had been fights. Where was Lake when she needed a significant other, or a *sig-oth* as Rita called it? She grabbed the paper bag from the twin that she didn't assault and checked it for her weapon.

"Pink gun." The other twin sneered and sauntered off with her clone.

"You're the one I should've hit you smug...cutie." She mumbled under her breath. With regrets she watched them sashay their fine asses away.

Outside task force headquarters news' vans unloaded personnel and equipment. The 7s Killer's—they ran with the name—recent escalation had finally chilled the press. Already he was being compared to Dahmer and Gacy, and blurred with the headhunter. The mix spun together piqued the taste buds of Chicagoland. Appetites were primed.

If it were Hollywood the violins and French horns would begin to play. Somebody was going to die. The audience was glued.

Lake hurried down the corridor towards Lindsey-Smith each step gobbling up real estate.

"Just checkin up on you. By the way, the press conference is happenin in bout thirty minutes." Lake repeatedly buttoned and unbuttoned the middle button of her pale white blazer.

In the short months that she had known Lake she had never

known her to fidget. She went on, gave Lake the details of her activity with the teenage geek and waited for the anger.

"If you get close enough shoot him in the head. Two shots. Double tap head shot. You feel me?" Lindsey-Smith hunched her shoulders and waited for the real Lake. "Double tap head shot. Say it. Double tap head shot."

"Double tap head shot." Lake searched her eyes. "I got it. I really do."

Lake unbuttoned. "Your eyes don't look right. I mean they're your eyes. But they're not. That makes no sense. Sorry."

"You in trouble, Lake?"

"Trouble's my middle name."

"Thought it was bitch."

"Don't fuck with me is my middle name, too." She buttoned.

"I got the idea."

"That wasn't meant for you." She unbuttoned almost ripping off the button.

"I kinda guessed that."

"Connors." She said it like a curse word.

He approached them from behind Lindsey-Smith. A heavy hand gripped her shoulder. She shook it off.

"Lindsey-Sm...Smith!"

Lindsey-Smith, her words damned up behind clenched teeth, pegged Connors for an uptight brotha. Tight compact muscles, his neck muscles bulged over a tight starched collar with a tie tight enough to lynch him if he sneezed. The tight military haircut belied his lack of military training. He spoke through thin pinched lips.

"You stay away from my crime scenes, Ms Smith. I'll arrest your ass if you compromise this investigation or department." He pivoted on a heel one hundred eighty degrees to Lake. "Next time she's under arrest." He assured her. He pivoted back to Lindsey-Smith but found Lake's body between them.

"She was just leavin." She said gently pushing Lindsey-Smith back. "Aren't you?"

She picked up the hint and backed up several steps then

took her thumb out of the dyke, "Strange a person can't keep away the demons he doesn't believe in." She strolled off.

Connors snapped. "What the hell does that mean, weirdo?" He sputtered unraveling. When he recovered a second later he moved to pursue her. With one quick giant step Lake blocked his path.

The hands-on by Connors had angered Lindsey-Smith. She could still feel where his fingers briefly dug into her shoulder. His intent clear—to hurt. Before she knew it anger had propelled her out the door and into the elevator. As the doors closed Lake stuck in an arm stopping the doors and startling Lindsey-Smith.

"Shit, Lake." She felt jumpy all over, that feeling she first got when the shadow appeared. For some reason that morning's near rear ender with a delivery van rattled her. "A rusty van pulled out in front of me and slammed on the brakes. Missed it by air bubbles. If I'd been in the Accord he would've been hit. That's how I feel bout Connors."

"Ignore him. My eyes are on him."

An undertone in Lake's voice that Lindsey-Smith couldn't name left her feeling uneasy like she missed something in the meaning of the statement. She let it go. "He's your problem. Thankfully, I don't have to listen to jack shit that oompa oompa butt says. Talkin bout irrelevant. You weren't checkin on my well being. Connors was comin after me and you knew it."

"I suspected. He's a bully. That's what a bully would do."

"Granted this is none of my business, but you miss Chief Boggs. I miss her for you."

The elevator stopped. Lake held the doors open. "What did that mean, what you said downstairs to Connors?"

"Whatever he wants it to mean." She half-smiled.

"Psych!" Lake roared as the elevator doors closed. Suddenly they opened. "Don't do that again. He's—"

Lindsey-Smith watched Lake's face clam up. The doors closed.

"Whoa!" Lake had suddenly turned into an odd sista. Not that she wanted her to talk office politics. Those thoughts vanished on the front steps of Task Force Headquarters.

48

Elston Avenue traffic turned into a four-lane parking lot with gapers eyeing familiar television reporters who clustered around Lindsey-Smith like she was somebody. Bold letters on microphones WGN, GAYDAR, ABC, WTTW, hovered predatorily around her mouth. She bared her teeth in an uncomfortable smile and pushed through the gaggle making a *B*-line for the Rover. Reporters' questions, nonetheless, registered with her and changed her point-of-view.

The cobwebs in her brain sagged.

Voices overlapped. "How did it feel to single-handedly bring down the headhunter?" "What were you doing at the raid?" "You've been on several crime scenes can you explain your presence." "Can you tell us about the kiss?" "Why do you carry a gun?"

There it was her chance. They were alabaster people in an alabaster world, laughable in a *Twilight Zone* kind of way.

She raised a hand and spoke in a whisper, which forced the group to quiet down. "I can't answer all those questions at once even though I'm sure you think I can cause you asked them all at once. So why don't I answer the questions I heard? I carry a gun cause musicians have lousy credit. But now that the world knows I won't be dealin in cash anymore. Plastic from here on." She lied, "And no gun." She adjusted the holster under her long black wool overcoat.

"Did you faint on Cindy Patron's body?" "Did you coin the name 7s Killer?" "How do you feel about saving Brenda Patron and then her getting murdered?"

"Yes and no."

"Yes you fainted on Cindy Patron's remains? "No you

didn't coin the name—" "No you know about the 7s killer investigation?"

She had them. Nobody asked the question she was about to answer; yet she doubted they would notice. She opened the car door to increase their urgency suckering them into thinking they were about to lose her. "I found it on the 7s killer's web page. The victims' names: Suzy, Sally, Betsey. All of em. There's a chant, *it's mine. You can't have it.* He's into picnics and mountains. Check it out." She slammed the door. Mountains? Thrust forward from the murky deep in her healed synapses, like an iceberg the image of mountains had sprung up from the gray sea.

In fact, she hadn't planned on saying the word *picnic.* Sure thing, Lake would misunderstand. *Picnic* was the word the task force used to describe the crime sites, perfect spots for intimate picnics. A red plaid blanket and straw picnic basket on the ground against the backdrop of forest-covered mountains had appeared when Lindsey-Smith repeated the names of the unknown victims.

A microphone tapped the windshield. A face got in the way.

She laid on the horn. It worked but not half as effectively as the Mac Truck horn installed in the Accord. She maneuvered around human roadblocks. "Get out of my way!" No matter how she turned it: inside out, upside down, Lake had shared the picnic theory with her warning her that the information had been kept away from the public. Now Lake's colleagues, Connors, fucking Connors would rip Lake a new one.

"I'm sorry, baby." Maybe Lake wouldn't believe her. That hadn't occurred to her. She dismissed the misgivings because there was nothing she could do about it now. The damage couldn't be undone. She had a better chance at un-ringing a bell.

In the process of turning right her right hand cramped. No matter how much she massaged and flexed the fingers it didn't alleviate the pain of a bone-crushing handshake, the kind that ring wearing studs serve when selling macho tickets to impress.

Intermittently, checking traffic, she examined her palm concluding she had a touch of arthritis. As she turned onto Devon she glanced down. On the back of her right hand lay the imprint of what appeared to be fingers. She felt them squeeze.

49

On cbsnews.com, streaming live, Tamara, the reporter, seemed pleased that she busted Deputy Chief Connors and the task force in general with news of the 7s Killer's web page. The names of alleged victims Suzy, Sally, and Betsey found on the web page drew blank looks from the task force a reporter from wgnnews.com, zestfully reported.

Gaydar.com reporter and talk show hostess, Prada, promised, after the nightly news at nine, an interview with Lindsey-Smith tagging her promise with *the kiss* will be one of the tough questions asked.

"I got something for your ass, Ms Smith." JP muttered at his I-POD as he rushed from the Illinois Unemployment Office. In the other hand, he clutched a plain white sheet of paper with a blood red stain in the center. He tossed it on the pavement where sunlight hit the paper and in bold black font ASZURE popped through the red marker. It fluttered into the gutter where it waved at passing motorists.

A woman's golden stiletto speared the paper. She spat at JP, "Trifflin" She rolled her eyes. Rolled her neck. Rolled her butt. "Trifflin!" And then crossed in front of the JP's van.

The van roared to life and jumped forward. He came that close. Close enough to shut her up. He shut down his self-destructive rage. The real culprit, the cunt he wanted to wipe out had upped the stakes with the web page that could've only been created by her. The police for their part, he couldn't be sure how she fit in with them. With Lieutenant Lake it was obvious after TV spread *the kiss* across the tube.

Lindsey-Smith had done the unthinkable. She had invaded

his brain and exposed it to the whole world for their abuse. No rip-off could be more intimate. Nothing was more private.

His visibility hung on his ritual. Its words exonerated and empowered him, delivered him from a slave's mentality on a mountaintop.

Not since then had he been so violated.

His nose bled.

His ears bled.

He took off his shirt and wiped away blood.

He kicked into another gear that evening from a perch on a windowsill leaning against a grimy window shade that had seen better days decades ago. The hovel of a rent-by-the-hour office had the same culture of tenants that supported the bam-bam thank you ma-dam hourly rate whore-motels surrounding it on Lincoln Avenue.

Prying his butt from the sill, he plopped it in a beat-up leather chair facing the window. He leaned back and locked his white cotton gloved fingers behind his shaved head.

A knock on the door broke his rapture.

He became somebody else.

Five locks required opening before a sunken-face black woman in her mid-twenties looking like sixty going strong entered with a shy girl. JP relocked all the locks including one that required a key, which he pocketed.

He had planned a later demise for the child before him but Lindsey-Smith pushed up the timetable. The girl's eyes found the lollipop on the desk. Joy twinkled in them when he handed her the lollipop, a caricature of her. She snatched it out of fear he would change his mind. The little girl broke into a snaggletooth smile as she ripped off the cellophane wrapper. First she licked and savored. She sucked noisily, and then bit off a chunk of her forehead. It gave JP pleasure to watch people turn into cannibals who would eat their own faces. Soon enough he made those real faces vanish.

The gaunt mother grinned flashing rotten teeth at JP, and then nudged the girl so hard she almost tipped over.

"Aszure, what you say?" The mother's head jerked stiffly

downward. "Show yo manners, girl. Say thanks to the nice man."

JP glanced down at the woman's broken filthy fingernails remembering the damage Brenda Patron had done to the back of his hands. "Let's get down to the sign up money?"

"What I have to sign?" Jittery, shifting around in the seat, she darted her eyes over the desk's surface until they landed on JP's forefinger that tapped on a one-inch locking plastic bag. Inside was a dirty white pebble. Suddenly bags spawned before her faulty eyes.

"In our experimental rehab program we want you to come in messed up so that we know your threshold. Everybody's is different, doncha know."

"Aight."

He pushed the bags across the desk to her. "Of course I understand if you decide this program isn't for you.... The bathroom's down the hall. I won't have you doin that in front of the little lady. We'll be here when you return. Take your time. Just sign first. Maybe your daughter would like a nice new white dress." At her hesitation he slowly pulled the bags towards him.

50

The Magnificent Mile pedestrian traffic had thinned to nightlife numbers and end of night shoppers. Lindsey-Smith scurried towards the Tribune Building. Her cell shouted out.

"Lindsey-Smith! What's up, Rita?" She collided with one of the Gold Coasts' beige ladies who cradled a beige dog to her beige bosom. "Sorry. Sorry." The dog snarled at her. "Shut up!" She yelled at the miniature dog. "No. Not you, girl." She upped her pace. "How'd you know? Yeah? It was on TV. Cool." She checked the time on her Movado. "Thanks for the warnin. But I need Prada more than she needs me." She entered mcdrop zone and loss the call.

With friends like Rita she didn't need stimulants. Rita injected adrenalin into whomever she interacted with. If Rita's call was an upper the next conversation was a downer, Lake jumped into her butt, spun her around, and then hustled her into the unmarked that she hadn't noticed pull up.

"I didn't leak the picnic to the press because I wasn't careful. What you told me had nothin to do with what I said. I have my own sources. Remember?" Lake shot off like Mentos in a bottle of soda. "Just...just listen for a minute would you."

"No, you listen. They wanted to kick me off the task force."

"Out of nowhere I saw these mountains and a picnic basket on a red plaid blanket."

"The only reason I'm still on the case is because the tips came to me. Connors can't afford to lose me."

"I saw Suzy."

"The Sup demoted me."

They locked eyes, "What did you say?" They asked in unison.

"You first."

"I saw Suzy at the picnic in the mountains. She had something he wanted really bad. Your turn. What did you say about bein demoted?" She asked hoping it wasn't true.

"I'm good." She said dismissively. "Tell me everything from the top."

"The pieces came together in a head on collision. This little boy was so happy smilin at a lollipop that favored him with big chocolate eyes and fat cherry cheeks. Except he's emaciated. Then that runnin through the forest barefooted. But these were little feet runnin from something. Little girls try to take his lollipop. One of them pulls on his penis cause he's wearin a raggedy white dress. He cries. He's looking at me. I can't help him. Then he's hysterical because a woman with a kitchen torch melts the lollipop. How could I...even for an instant, how could I feel so terrible that I couldn't protect that boy?"

"That little boy was him, the killer as a boy, you know. My God, baby, your memory's back. That had to be the seminal event. The thing that started the whole thing. The thing that lead to all this carnage. Could you see Suzy well enough to describe her?"

"Not really. But I'd know her eyes."

"What color are they?"

"White."

"Her eyes. What color are her eyes?" Lindsey-Smith didn't answer. "Okay, tell me why her eyes are white."

"Everything in his world is a shade of white." She checked her watch. "Show time." She wiggled out of the seat. Lake grabbed her hand detaining her. "Think before you speak, for God's sake. This could back fire."

"It's my turn. I have to take it. You gonna catch the show? It's Pod-cast. Just in case, I TiVo'd it." She disembarked in a big hurry.

Lake shouted, "I'll be watchin in Millennium Park over coffee. Break a leg."

Barbara J. Wells

Lindsey-Smith shouted over her shoulder, "Pick me up right here." As she broke into a half-trot she realized that having Lake around was reassuring. She was the only constant.

51

Broadcast from the Tribune Building, overlooking the Chicago River, Gaydar's studio was barebones, two high-back chrome stools—one of which held Lindsey-Smith—and a black and red logo used as a backdrop. In her opinion, one word, boring. But on television the studio, no doubt because of tight shots, appeared contemporary.

The songwriter hummed a melody as she checked out the studio behind sunglasses worn to hide her black, blue and orange eyes from the camera. She felt the woman before seeing her. Prada rode in on an energetic smile that would set off anybody's gaydar. The woman had her lesbian persona down flat. Not your usual lesbian came to Lindsey-Smith's mind as she inspected for flaws she could exploit.

The five foot tall fashionista's hair bounced as she gave orders and received them in an unending ebb and flow of crew and staff. Lindsey-Smith saw what Rita was talking about. Prada threw knives, mostly at backs. She made a note not to turn her back on Prada unless she was sitting on her face.

As if hearing her thoughts the hostess stopped talking and scrutinized her face. "Take off your sunglasses. That beat-down look sells." Not prone to following orders, Lindsey-Smith hesitated. "I know you must be wondering who the fuck am I to tell you what to do? Baby, if you want people to listen to you, you gotta have a hook in this industry. The camera is everything. What you have to say means very little. This is a visual industry. Otherwise, it's radio." Lindsey-Smith removed the sunglasses. "Dedicate a camera to her face."

A forced smile split Lindsey-Smith's lips. The bursitis in her hand squeezed. She was feeling as up tight as Connors looked when she snapped on him. Focus. She reminded herself she had two goals to meet on the show: to spread the word about the 7s Killer's web page in order to increase the possibility of him seeing it and coming after her; to expose his cold cases to which she was positive the old fashion names Suzy, Betsey, and Sally were attached—he had began every killing with those names. She had no choice but to accept them as if they once existed. And if they did, somebody had to remember them. She couldn't imagine a town forgetting about its murdered children.

"Let's get to it." She turned to the camera and spoke. "Hi, I'm Prada and this is Lindsey-Smith Cutter. A fledging songwriter, a masters in blah blah blah...do you care? This you might care about."

Lindsey-Smith steeled her eyes keeping them unreadable while in her head she wanted to hammer the hostess for digging into her background like any of it mattered to the world. For the killer it would be fodder, for her, clearly unintended consequences. For them she hadn't planned.

Prada continued. "Recently, she received a contract to write a love song for blah blah blah....DVD scheduled to drop this spring..."

Lindsey-Smith shifted uneasily on her stool. She hooked her heels over the rung.

"Recently, this past September, she awarded a group of second-graders full scholarships through college. A few days ago she saved a woman from a serial killer." She turned to Lindsey-Smith, "My hero, let's start with that. And then we'll talk about *the kiss* with that Mchottie lieutenant...," a shot of the kiss popped up as an insert on a studio TV monitor, "... that's gettin lots of hits on U-TUBE." She positively preened.

"We'll talk about *the kiss* first." Lindsey-Smith caught the look of disapproval in Prada's eyes. "Please, give that hero title to Chief Boggs. I saw the building comin down over Lieutenant Lake's shoulder so I told her to run. Wouldn't you kiss someone who just saved your life?"

"Not like that."

"If they saved your life I suspect you'd kiss them anyway they liked."

"You have a point." Then she regained control of the interview. "The police hid the fact that you killed a serial killer for them. Talk about that."

"They hid nothin. The man fell on his own knife when he was tryin to kill me."

"If I might point out...you helped him get there. They didn't. The horror of eight decapitated heads." She shivered for effect. "How do you sleep?"

The hot seat victim didn't notice that she was wiping her hands on her lavender wool slacks. "I don't. When my eyes close I see my hand pick up a decomposing head and stuff it in a man's face. Sleep? A pedophile is killin our children. Go on his web page and see the names. Suzy. And Betsey. And Sally."

Action.

In that achromatic concave universe where JP thrived and in Lindsey-Smith's mind she screamed *NO* when she saw herself on an I-POD placed above the head of a girl who lay at the foot of a thick tree. Her wide eyes blinked twice.

Oh, little girl. Sweetheart, I'm so sorry I can't help you. But the words couldn't get pass her tongue which she found stuck at the roof of her mouth.

Lindsey-Smith's eyes cut back to her image on the I-POD. Frozen like a stalk of broccoli. She saw Prada standing over her frantically gesturing to someone off stage. Lindsey-Smith's brain screamed, *cut the fuckin' cameras, be'atch.* Reality TV had fallen into Prada's lap and Lindsey-Smith was performing a lap dance without busting a move. A job had to be performed that only she could do. Still looking for a clue that would lead to the killer she stopped the unhinging that threatened to ruin everything.

In search of the GPS Lindsey-Smith eyes shifted to the man's left wrist.

It went blank, her world black.

As she adjusted her body into a sitting position it occurred to her she was on the floor with a fresh headache. A real dozy.

Her fingers located a burning lump forming on her forehead. "Not my head again."

"Are you all right, Ms Cutter?" A strictly business voice inquired.

"How did I get down here?" Shakily, she rose to her feet. "And what happened to my head." Guilty faces around her all looked to Prada for guidance.

Lindsey-Smith pushed through them. A little girl was dead and it was her fault. Yet here she was asking irrelevant questions of fools when she should be warning Lake that the 7s Killer had struck again.

52

In a panic Lindsey-Smith darted from the Tribune Building next to which she felt like an ant under the spike heel of a ho about to take a hard stroll on its back. She scooted across Michigan Avenue. A car horn blasted her into the moment. She headed south. Cherry pickers putting up Christmas lights dotted the street like giant dwarfs.

"Where are you, Lake?" She looked up and down the street. Chicago was white all over and it hadn't snowed. In its splendor, the Mag Mile, of white on white, platinum on alabaster, oyster and bone, pearl against chalk, ivory and milky bent against the curve in her imagination.

She decided it unwise to stand on the street looking like one of those people who frequent downtown to express their insanity. She rushed south to the bridge over Chicago River, which ran as backwards as things had just turned in her life. She didn't know the child's name or where to find her body. It was a step backwards, a giant one. Time was running out, not backward.

The still black sheet of water reflected lights from streets and buildings surrounding it. It seemed a moving painting by Monet. She was tempted to reach in and touch it to see if the paint was wet.

She leaned over the railing.

She felt the water lap against her fingertips.

Fingers tightened around her hand. They pulled her downward.

"What're you doin?" Lake asked snatching her back.

She raised her dripping wet hand watching the water roll down her arm before shaking it off. Several drops splashed against Lake's cheek and left in their wet path, incredulity, confusion, disbelief, and then belief staged on her face. Lake shot a fearful look at the river—three stories below them—and pulled Lindsey-Smith away down the sidewalk. "You touched the water. No way. How?" The lieutenant Lake grabbed her arm, "I saw you go into a trance of some kind. Lindsey, answer me, damn it. Did you?"

"Until I stop him I'm stuck in his head, you know. Every time he kills a girl, I'll be there. That little girl died thinkin I killed her. She's right. I killed her. I killed that baby. My stupid idea got her killed."

"Stop it! She couldn't see you."

"I don't know where she is, Lake. Something happened and I got disconnected..." She paused as pedestrians brushed by them. "I disconnected from the wishscape before he killed her. He wasn't wearin the GPS though. That much I know."

They moved quickly towards the privacy of the unmarked parked on the other side of the bridge, warning signals went off. The bridge was going up.

"There can be no doubt that he knows you're connected to him some way. He set you up. You thought you were setting him up. He figured out how we found the last two girls so fast. And now ol boy knows bout you. Knows you freeze up when he offends. No way could he miss that. He knows you're the one who'll bring him down. He can't let you live."

"He killed that girl to study me."

Lake didn't make it better with consoling remarks. "You wanted him to come after you. He's never gonna do what you want him to do."

"He's comin after me." She insisted.

"Maybe."

"It's his nature, the way his brain works."

"What's this with you adoptin a second-grade class?"

"How could I forget?" She sagged. "You have to protect them, Lake. I mean, it won't be too hard for him to find out who they are. It's public record you know."

"So you can't be too poor. Just how do you adopt what, twenty-two second graders through college?"

"Long story. Talkin bout it won't protect them. And it definitely won't find her body."

"Nothins gonna find her remains anytime soon. Chicagoland has hectares of woods. Even with cadaver dogs it would take weeks to check out all them. And with just one CPD helicopter with thermal imagin capabilities and the night's temperature droppin the window to find the body while it's still warm is vanishin the closer tomorrow gets to today."

"You could at least try it."

"I can't try anything. I'm not lead investigator. I'm sorry. Give me the names of the seven-year old girls in your class."

"You got it. This is bad, Lake. Can't you find a way round Connors I mean?"

"Forget it. Consider him just another obstacle. Jump the fuck over it. Move on, baby. I really believe we have no choice here."

And they didn't. They were stuck waiting for the bridge to go up and down—in the city with the most movable bridges in the world—over the only river in the world that ran backwards.

"We need to drop the tip, Lindsey. Nothin changes on that score. Well, except you can't make this call. The fibbers are recordin all the calls to my cell, remember?"

"I know someone who'll make the call." She punched out a phone call as the bridge rose above her spreading its platinum legs to the frosted white night sky.

"The moon has a beautiful red cast." Lake observed.

53

Fifteen minutes after killing Aszure JP found himself stuck in a tunnel on a freeway in downtown Chicago behind an accident. Stuck there he felt his own demise. Claustrophobia smothered him just as it had in that truck in the desert in which the coyotes locked and abandoned him and his parents and several dozen others. A piece of him had been stolen; a piece he could never get back.

Pieces had been exposed by Lindsey-Smith. Names had been spoken, names that could lead to high school pictures of him. Back then he hadn't been very careful or clever. The cops had ways to digitally age photos. The coroners might have saved his DNA. He had no reason not to believe they would also go so far as to determine his ethnicity since he had made it an issue with his disguises and race bending with victims' mothers.

The time was now. He had to get the fuck up out of Dodge ASAP. His van got smaller. He lowered both windows. For the moment, like a bunch of others in that tunnel, he was going nowhere.

"Cool." He settled in studying a recording of Lindsey-Smith's abbreviated *Gaydar* interview. A simple death was no longer enough. The highest payment he could exact from any human lay in the right torture. To him torture was intimacy at its best. Like everything else, you had to enjoy it to be good at it.

For that he took their children. Suzy, Betsey, and Sally were relatives of people who did him wrong. The other girls were substitutes for them. As he watched the short interview he discovered all that he needed. For the first time he had heard her full name. Till now he thought that Smith was her last name. On the TV screen *Gaydar* hyphenated Lindsey-Smith. He figured it for her songwriter name. The name Cutter presented another option. Could it be? It wouldn't take long to find out. He giggled, and then goggled her. The tunnel denied him, refused to give him a signal.

"Fuck!" He smacked the steering wheel.

54

Rita's Place, a lesbian bar, sizzled with New Orleans style décor, ceiling to floor bright colored oil paintings of Amazon blues and jazz female singers with nipples and discreet nude buttocks peeping through see through fabrics. Here and there the triumphal arch between their legs left telling outlines against the fabric's shadow. Mini spotlights highlighted the areas.

Lindsey-Smith had come seeking the one person who she trusted to help them with calling in the tip. Rita was a friend and a performer. Damn good at both in Lindsey-Smith's eyes.

She had arrived in the middle of Rita's comedy routine, infamously called *Passion for Pussy*. It was comedy night. Only women were welcomed to get on stage and do their funny thing. Rita always closed the show, which is what she was doing now.

There wasn't a black face in the place Lindsey-Smith noticed.

Rita's huge slightly cracked voice and easy New Orleans's accent stitched the crowd to a slow southern delivery.

"One more thang bout diva pussy. If you aint had it you don't know what Ahm talkin bout. If you had it, shut up. Diva pussy loves tongue, hot wet tongues. It sees a woman and immediately moans, 'Ah want yo mouth'. But what *she* says is, 'you have a pretty smile.'" With a huge smile Rita strolled on the stage. "You know who you are."

She stopped suddenly, made a face of disgust and shivered from hair to hips. "What aint diva pussy? Yall knows who you are." She smiled broadly. "For those who don't know, one more thang bout tired pussy. You know, lazy pussy. It don't work. Just like lazy people, you aint gonna convince it to work. E-ver. Stop trippin." She smiled.

Above her head she held a forefinger ringed with silver, "One last thang bout pussy passion." She took a drink from a customer and slipped in three inches of tongue touching bottom then stirred. "One last thang. Ahm talkin very last. You ever meet a woman and she say, 'baby, Ah love havin ma pussy eaten?'" She smiled. "Be suspicious. Lesbians don't say that cause it's a given, by fuckin definition. But just in case, check it out. You go in there first thang. You find ridges on them walls means that pussy's been rollin plenty dick. That's why it's got calluses. Walk away, baby. Walk away like this." She ran off the stage. Laughter trailed behind her.

On the far side of the L-shaped bar a door led to a flight of stairs and Rita's loft. She unlocked the door and motioned Lindsey-Smith to precede her.

"Place got security cameras installed this mornin. Look up. Caint tell they're there."

Lindsey-Smith headed for a chocolate leather couch, but came up short preferring to stand. The ride over with the siren screaming had jarred her ribcage into searing anger to match her headache. She felt like one big impacted wisdom tooth. The sucking couch would be her last call.

"Something wrong, cheri?" Rita's tone said she had no doubt that something was wrong.

"Three cracked ribs."

"Like havin a paper cut on yo eyeballs!"

Lindsey-Smith tugged at the Ace Bandage gaining little relief from the snug fabric that shafted her skin. Rita gently laid a hand against her friend's torso, "Ah mean yo eyes. You keep battin them. And pumpin yo hand."

"Ah need a favor."

"Watcha need, daddy?"

No hesitation. No questions. She would do anything for Lindsey-Smith. She was a friend. "Need you to make a phone call."

"Done."

"You'll be breakin the law." She warned.

"If it aint murder...."

"It is murder."

"Jesus Lord." Rita flopped on the couch.

After the call Lindsey-Smith, concerned about exposing Rita to a child killer, watched her lean back to gather herself. Her big thighs spread apart to allow her be-ringed fingers to form a cradle in her plush lap. It always reminded Lindsey-Smith of hands at the ready to give a person a step up—over the fence—for she had used them that way to save lives during the days after Katrina. People were alive because of that cradle and those big thighs. Lindsey-Smith rubbed her nose. It was her loss that she couldn't get with that.

"Now what?"

"We wait."

"Who is she? And why haven't Ah met my competition?"

"Careful. I'm not a doctor." Lindsey-Smith noticed that Rita lost some of that southern tilt in her accent when she got off stage.

"You know there are always exceptions to the rule. So who is she? Wait a hot minute. Not that detective? She's like a cat. That one'll devour you."

"We were meant to meet."

"I can't believe you just laid that old lesbian myth on me." She touched Lindsey-Smith's thigh and gave it a sympathetic pat. "Ah need a drink. Too bad you're allergic to alcohol. Ah suspect you could use five or six shots."

"I mean she's in my life for a reason. That cold hand of evil you felt when you were makin the call maybe it's me."

"Ah refuse to believe that."

"You and I were meant to meet. My whole life...."

"Was meant to be."

"I was thinkin more along the lines of my life is a set-up."

"So you have no free will you're tellin me? You been dabblin in voodoo?" Rita took Lindsey-Smith's face in her hands. "Lordy. What are you involved in?"

"Figured you could see it."

Rita pulled Lindsey-Smith into her sumptuous EE breasts wrapping pillow bare arms protectively around her.

She spoke into Rita's core. "That cold hand of evil...it's all over me. It's like a shadow on my soul, a greasy coal stain on what's good in me." She sighed. Her hot breath spread between Rita's cleavages. They sat; Lindsey-Smith emitted a squeal between clinched teeth. "One night I went to this bar that I basically didn't like. It was before your time. CK's and Augies. Anyway, the only openin I could find to get a drink at the bar was the barmaid island. A blond man was sittin to the right of it. Right off I noticed he was wearin a cheap white short sleeve shirt. That was a clue. He had to be straight. I checked the mirror and saw this weirdo's reflection seriously turkey neckin. He had these big blank hazel eyes, like a corgi's, starin at something beyond the mirror. His arm was like a lever that kept liftin a dark drink to his mouth. A black feelin like evil and death walkin hand-in-hand shot through me. I jumped back two feet right into the barmaid who I yelled at askin why they let a straight man in. She just smiled no worries when she said he's got no straight bars to go to round here. I shot back if Carol were alive his ass wouldn't be in here. But he's real nice she said. I said fuck that, right he aint. And got the hell out of there. But it really messed with me that nobody else in that packed bar felt what I felt."

She removed a folded piece of paper from a back pocket and handed it to her friend, "That photo was in a crime book an ex gave me. I think that witch made it fall open on that page. It's shot at the same angle I had of Dahmer that night. One degree of separation. That was the beginnin. I just didn't know it at the time. Every weekday mornin when I walked my dog we would see this pleasant laid back gay man who we developed a good-mornin relationship with. Then one day he wasn't there. A month went by. Two months. I figured he moved. Then posters went up about a missin person with this matchbook size black and white photo that I recognized immediately. It was the good-mornin guy. At the time I thought he was white. Months later I read he was bi-racial when they listed him as one of Jeffery Dahmer's victims. Come to think of it, Dahmer drank the way these old coots drank in this tavern where all this shit started."

"What tavern?"

"How many degrees of separation are there when you stand centimeters from a serial killer and his victim, maybe even on the day they connected?"

"What tavern?"

"Forget it. It doesn't exist."

"Funny thing. Suga, that don't make you a serial killer magnet."

"My life is a set-up. When I was a kid my cousin's boyfriend was workin at his father's furniture store when Gacy came in and asked to use the phone. It seems he had cut the phone wires while working on the plumbing at the drug store across the street. The way he tells it, for bout a half hour, til the phone company arrived, Gacy held a normal, if not easy goin conversation with him. Two weeks later, cuz was the person he ran to all bent out of shape when he saw John Wayne Gacy being arrested on TV. She said when he told the story and for a long time afterwards he looked like a broken man because he'd come so close to evil and didn't recognize it. He kept repeatin that Gacy seemed perfectly normal; like if he said it enough he'd spot the evil he missed durin their conversation. How many degrees of separation is that for me?"

"That don't make yo life a set-up."

"Two years later my baby sister was taken. You know, I will always believe that it was my fault. Nobody can take that away from me. The police believed it was the work of a serial killer who was probably passin through. Just passin through." She sighed. "Passin' through cause there were no other reports of missin kids. How many degrees? C'mon. And now the 7s Killer."

"It aint a set-up. It's called comin full circle."

Lindsey-Smith climbed to her feet, groaning, "The circle needs to be broken before it hangs me."

"Take care of it, cheri."

55

10:06 p.m. Halloween. PCH.

Jass, unaware she was missing her first helicopter ride, felt hands strap her body in bondage. But they couldn't make her release the energy onto which she held for dear life. She squeezed the hand.

"Incubate!" A sharp shout above the sound of the chopper's blades swish-chop-swash; forced—a cold object down Jass's throat. She struggled against the object delivering oxygen.

"Breathe!"

Why are you screamin at me? You don't know me like that. She held her breath.

"She's gone. Call it." Wind driven horizontal rain beat the battered helicopter off its course towards the fierce mountain that the ex-Iraq Blackhawk pilot maneuvered to avoid as if under enemy attack, but howling gusts swooping around the mountain swatted the Med Vac against the mountain side, blades first. They broke off spinning and chopping into cars and occupants.

The chopper exploded into a conflagration, raining red hot metal, melted plastic, melted limbs, and Jass—her heart jump-started by the crash—like scree on the highway and Halloween night travelers.

At that moment time stood still or at least in Jass's unconscious brain it was so. Nonetheless, she embraced the comforting notion. There were no absurdities in the unconscious world. Pain receded to nothingness.

Thorny claws pulled Jass's body from the conflagration; unable to struggle free she formed words that found no escape. Her ears processed the rasping voice that belonged to Dracula's twisted neck companion who repeatedly asked Jass, "Do you believe time stands still?" Each time the creature asked its voice grew primordial.

Jass' eyes blinked open and saw thorny claws ripping away her burning clothes, a blue hyena toiled in the fire in her hair, and a red woman with snake hair stuck something in her mouth. Her brain registered the awful penetration. She hated penetration in any form.

She tried to spit it out.

Exhaustion overwhelmed her as those who wanted her to live and those who demanded she die fought. The thorny claws of the alligator removed its head and administered CPR. The rain stopped. Skies cleared. The half moon appeared and frigid stars sparkled more than hot diamonds. A praying constellation turned its back.

The devil's minions welcomed Jass who ran backwards legless. Her hand held on tightly to the hand that she couldn't see, but feel its strength she could.

56

Satan's human mentor readied his spine; eager to take his place at Satan's left.

"Condemnment six!"

"But...but there are only five condemnments." His voice quivered for he dared to question Satan, second only to God.

Satan roared shooting a barrage of comets from his eyes across the universe towards earth unleashing solar radio bursts that affected every Global Positioning System receiver on the lighted half of the earth completely destroying their ability to determine position.

"Condemnment six! Stand to my right!"

His human mentor groveled, "To your right? Master, most noble one, that's ov...over the black hole. I'll get sucked into hell. I've satisfied all of your condemnments. The courageous souls—your fav tasty treat—I brung em to your feast. Surely—" He gulped.

Satan snatched his human mentor by his scrawny neck, turned him around, bent him over, and fucked him inside out.

"You a minion now, muthafucka."

57

Shadows do not cast without light.

It must be true Lindsey-Smith decided as she rocked back and forth on the end of the rumpled sleigh bed gripping her achy swollen hand and watching the morning local news beat up on the Special Task Force Department. Lieutenant Kyniska Lake's name was mentioned more than a few times, and *the kiss* was still news, though not half as salacious as the 7s Killer. But somehow the recipient of that kiss might be the reason the former lead investigator couldn't do her job.

She felt compelled to stick up for Lake who had been incommunicado all night leaving her hanging until the wee hours of the morning when she reported the police helicopter had discovered the remains of a girl.

The M.E. placed the T.O.D. between nine-fifty and ten-fifty the previous night. Lindsey-Smith gave Lake the exact time of death, three minutes after ten. Before the window closed on their conversation, with seconds left before they were cut off, she managed to tell Lake what she saw through the killer's twisted eyesight: Suzy picking up something from the forest floor too miniaturized for her to see what it was.

An image on the plasma screen intrigued her. She turned up the volume. The woman speaking to the reporter had a face that brought the word *melted* to Lindsey-Smith's mind. No nose eyebrows eyelashes eyelids. Stuck in perfect earlobes were one-carat diamond studs. The melted lady spoke through a face without lips.

"The man who did this to me twenty years ago has attacked five women since then. The last one on Halloween night. Berlin

Turnbol did not survive. How many victims does it take before the task force considers a crime the work of a serial?"

From the looks of things the task force was going to have its hands full for the press conference called for that morning. If she was waiting for it she surmised the 7s Killer would also be waiting to see what the police and FBI recently learned from California about him.

Lake had been unable to update Lindsey-Smith but based on the adrenalin rush in Lake's voice something was up. At least she had been able to insure the safety of the three girls in Lindsey-Smith's second-grade class with sibilants in their names. She could only assume that it wasn't accomplished with the help of the Chicago Police Department.

The next image shocked her. It was an exterior shot of the school where her second-graders attended. Vigorously shaking her aching hand she pulled herself to her feet. She saw the shit hit the fan before it did.

Outside the school a minister and his congregation marched against the Board of Education. The reverend preached, "Irate God-fearin parents have filled my e-mail askin the church not to allow a lesbian to bring her ways to our children. She used scholarships, yes she did. She used scholarships to get next to our children to make them think homosexuals are okay." In the background, arriving students waved and clowned for the camera. Most arriving parents didn't have a clue about the controversy, but agreed with the minister.

As she could have predicted eight seconds earlier, her students disembarked from one of the school buses on the street.

"Keep walkin." She shouted at the plasma screen. But her students didn't. Not when they heard the preacher's demand: take back the scholarships.

Her frightened, but amazing students paraded in front of the camera and defended her with the straightforward wisdom of children. She shook her head. There should be a law against interviewing children without their parents being present. On some levels she considered the behavior abusive. She made note of the reporter's name.

Suddenly she had a reversal of hope. She hoped the beast wasn't watching, after all. She didn't want his evil eyes on her children. The thought of it sickened her down to knees that cascaded to the floor like a banana peel squishing open extruding the electric nightmare in which she knelt uselessly in prayer, a constellation above her Muslim child watching her kicked to death by classmates.

For support she leaned against the bed, watched the camera shot follow her children into the school as the reporter shot off his mouth off camera. The reporter asked, "The question is how an unsuccessful song writer pays for twenty-two cradle to bachelors' scholarships?"

There it was; the other shoe had dropped. The last thing on earth that she wanted was to have Serena's name connected with the sordid mess she was in. And she never wanted attention for the way she used the monies she inherited from her sister's death. Invested by her parents, the money had amassed a fortune by the time she turned twenty-one and refused to ever touch it.

In the bathroom where she found herself ten minutes later, she dared take an assessment of her face. Her rocky face, pitted with bruises and scratches, cuts and stitches now had a big fat *g* for guilty written across it. To run with the story the press would dig up her sister's life and death. She worried about her parents, her mother in particular. It would devastate them to have Serena's goodwill slammed.

The TV alerted her. The press conference had begun. A picture of the murdered child's face in-situ splashed on the screen when she pulled up in front of it.

"C'mon, you bastard. Come after me. I'm the one you should fear." She went to her closet and opened the safe. From here on she would wear pinky. *Double tap headshot* ran through her mind as she strapped on the holster. She checked the ammunition.

59.

JP unlocked his office door.

The press conference did not go well.

In his mind the press should have pushed questions about the person leaving the tips after the police played a recording of the tape hoping someone recognized the voice.

It was not Lindsey-Smith's voice. It wasn't Lake's either. He had recordings of their voices. It was some dude's voice, which meant there was another player. That irked his backside. Maybe someone would recognize the gruff voice and turn it in for the reward. If it happened he'd take the voice out, too. Just for the fuck of it. He sucked on his rage.

"Dumb ass cops."

The task force had been unable to trace the website back to the unknown black woman who paid cash to set it up. Apparently, she hired a teenager who described the person as too stupid to do it herself.

He felt like getting into his tonic to maintain control.

It was over. His long ass run was *finito*.

They had his fingerprints, his DNA from California and a photograph from his high school yearbook digitally aged. Most disturbing, the DNA evidence found on Brenda Patron's jeans matched the California DNA.

"You fuckin' cunt!" The man couldn't believe he let her out think him.

Even plan *B* was now in jeopardy. Somebody was bound to eventually recognize him if he stuck around with his undisguised face on display at work. It was just a matter of time. If he left now his face would be out of sight. He went to plan C—murder and mayhem—to insure he came out whole. That meant he would remain eligible for his poppy's pension.

The task force even promised they would learn his ethnicity through DNA. They were awaiting the results. JP giggled. It turned to rage. "I'm the trifecta, mothafucka. What the hell do you mean who am I? I'm black from Belize, Mexican from Mexico, and white from the shores of America. You know me. I'm the face of your newest slave trade. How do you like me now?"

A face in the crowd of students he saw on TV pulled him back from the brink.

Had he not goggled Lindsey-Smith and sent out mass e-mails to churches in the second-graders' communities he wouldn't have seen that face. He knew who Lindsey-Smith Cutter was and now he knew why she adopted that second grade class.

"You'll pay. You'll pay higher than anyone ever has just to show you how I feel bout you."

He rushed from the Unemployment Office without consulting Prince knowing it would turn him on to write him up. In a couple of hours it wouldn't matter.

The workman's compensation doctor's waiting room was packed tight as a scam of petty thieves. The orange Formica walls and worn floor gave testament to the dull intellect of bureaucracy.

JP walked into a psychiatrist's office without an appointment. The doctor, fresh out of medical school turned his attention on JP's briefcase which opened with a *click*.

"Hello Plan *B*. Your student loan is four hundred and thirty-six thou. There's four times that in there. If you count it, I'll smack you. You have seven seconds to say *yes* and live. Or say *no* and die with your integrity and cripplin debt in tact. All I want is out of work nine months early. Seven six—."

"You are the most depressed patient I've seen in my er... career. Classic. I'm gonna write some prescriptions. Fill them when they're due. If you don't, it would be a mistake. The medicines costly, but you're insured. Are you gonna shoot me or whatever?"

"You'll be round to keep this paper work goin."

"I can't pay my loan off. It'll draw the wrong kind of attention. You know that, don't you?"

"I'm glad you're a wise one. Means I won't have to come back to correct you." He made himself smile.

The smile sent the doctor into a swoon. When he recovered he adjusted his eyeglasses and croaked, "You don't have to answer this, and it's optional. What ethnicity are you?"

"White."

"I can tell by the way you talk. Black and Latino accents always tell on em."

"Is that so?" JP tried to smile but couldn't muster one. He would love to kill the supercilious bigot but needed him more than the sour cherry taste of death.

Back at his office, JP propped his briefcase on the desk and opened it. He removed a burned, melted lollipop, a disfigured caricature face of a boy from long ago. Carefully he removed the clear cellophane and ran a finger across the candy face. He saw it, as it once was—bright colors—when chef made it for his twelfth birthday present, the first he had ever received. It looked like a happy him.

Then the little rich bitch's mother trapped him back at the house not knowing what he had done, but out of evil spite, melted his lollipop with the chef's torch.

He grabbed a kitchen knife and cut the back of her knees. She collapsed. On the way down the torch flamed her hair and nightgown. She roasted and he watched enjoying the smells and screams. To prevent her from crawling out to the pool he locked the door. When she stopped burning he picked up his lollipop and wrapped it in cellophane that long ago yellowed and cracked, like his nightmares.

From a locked office drawer he removed the green jar filled with a bouquet of lollipops.

"Times up, suckas."

His tiny office turned oppressive when the gaudy one entered soaked in a suffocating gardenia perfume. The smell was synonymous with southern California where they grew in bunches. He detested the overwhelming cloying fragrance and the woman who wore it.

The woman smiled around a long hooked nose and through a canyon between her front teeth. It was a comforting smile except to JP.

He sneezed without covering his mouth.

"You said you were gonna make a sucker of me. Uh oh. I forget. You don't like people callin them suckers." Her Brooklyn accent embraced the room.

"Have a sucker."

"Really?" She dove into the bouquet and found her face. "Did you see how the snow's comin down? It sure wasn't predicted."

JP followed her to the office door and looked out. It was snowing big fat fluffy flakes.

"Doesn't look like it's stickin, thank God. I am so not prepared." She looked down at new alligator pumps. "I rather walk barefooted. Don't think I won't."

"Don't think I care." He ducked back in the office and grabbed the lollipops and passed them out. In Prince's office he bowed and scraped then dropped his workmen compensation papers on the desk.

Prince perused the paperwork, and then flung it aside. "Great! I love it. You're out of here. Priest, too bad I didn't have the pleasure of messin up your pension. I was this close."

JP laid a sucker on top of the papers. "You still got the Leno chin."

Prince ripped off the cellophane. "Pretend this is you." And bit off the head. JP about-faced and exited the office. A woman's whopping screams signaled death had started. Prince shoved by him. JP re-entered the office and removed the sucker leaving another from which a piece was broken as if it had been bitten off.

Staff raced from offices and cubicles to the front of the office and crowded around the gardenia lady as she lay writhing on the floor drooling foam.

To eleven offices and cubicles JP made a visit, collecting and leaving half eaten suckers. Then he removed himself from the building leaving behind the growing hysteria to pursue the rest of his life.

60

Lindsey-Smith, trying to work through the tightness and weakness developing in her hand played several chords on the piano. Lake sat next to her on the piano bench perhaps to watch her hands since she was tone deaf and the notes sounded all the same.

"You held your own. Connors showed his ass in front of TV-land."

"He doesn't even get that he did that."

"The man's got a little Hitler in him." She did runs in the muddy bass notes. "They must have tried to move me. Sorry, I jumped subjects. But it just hit me." She banged. "The people at Gaydar dropped me on my head. When they cut to commercials they tried to move me. That's how I hit my head. And *that's* why I disconnected from the transfixion. Do you see what that means? I can control it...with some help."

"Don't ask me to knock you out."

"Yeah. That won't work. But anything that alters my brain waves would work."

"Booze."

"Allergic."

"Whatever you come up with you'll have to be already under the influence when he attacks. In which case, you might not go under at all...when he attacks."

"I don't have answers. But I need one real soon." Lake stilled her hand clinching hand with a light touch of her fingertips. Lindsey-Smith flinched.

"Your hand looks terrible. That's the strangest rash. It's in the shape of long thin fingers."

"I noticed." She hit high *A*-sharp. "It works in my favor,

the press conference. Go'damn sonafbitch's feelin the pressure. Know he hates my black ass."

"We know the region his Mexican mother came from. Aint DNA wonderful. Bet he aint livin black as an adult." Without being asked Lindsey-Smith's fingers played the partial melody of the song that didn't stand a chance on being finished. "He must have lived as black at some time growin up cause he knows the culture. Otherwise, you know he wouldn't be able to fool the black mothers. Unless he's suddenly gone stupid he knows we're gettin close. We have his DNA. Latent prints. And a digitally aged photograph."

"Which doesn't help since he wears disguises."

"They don't live day to day in disguise."

"See. You survived the news conference with a single bruise. Thought you were goin down didn't you?"

"Had a natural shield bein the only one in that room that knew the perp's clock *is* tickin. The FBI's been all over Rita's voice, by-the-by." She worried.

Lindsey-Smith took Lake by the hand. "No problem. She used one of her comedy voices she hasn't used in decades." Unusual for Lake she followed without question. "C'mon, I want to show you the tickin clock." Lindsey-Smith said explaining herself anyway as she led Lake into the studio bathroom.

Surrounded by mirrored walls Lindsey-Smith leaned over the clear glass bowl sink. Lake did likewise. They both stared at her reflection. She removed the bandage on her cheek. .

"Do you see any redness?"

Lake looked at her long and hard. "Yes. Why are you askin me?"

"Everything I see is white. Shades of white, technically." The arching eyebrow showed Lake clearly didn't understand. "You're white." Lake's jaw dropped. She was beginning to believe. "Your hair is white. Your eyes are white. You're white."

"Trick or treat."

"What kind of response is that?"

She grabbed Lindsey-Smith's shoulders and shook them. "Your Halloween wish. Trick or treat? Which is it?"

"So far *trick* is winnin. I can see a little pale color around the edges of my vision. Hour by hour the world round me gets whiter and whiter. When the color's all gone, it begins. The last lap. White's the color of his sordid world."

"How...how long? How long before you go white?" She gripped harder.

"Ouch, Lake! Maybe two. Could be three."

"Months? Weeks?" Aghast, Lake stepped back. "Days."

Lindsey-Smith looked in the mirror at Lake's reflection. "Hours, baby. Tick fuckin tock."

"I'm not leavin your side." She pulled Lindsey-Smith into her arms and smothered her.

The bathroom phone rang breaking the raw silence. Lindsey-Smith read the caller ID then picked up. "Hi, sweetie," covering the mouthpiece, "my mom." She forced happy in her tone, "Not yet. Beats me why the Rover breaks down so much. But, yeah, it's doin that, not bad enough to break down I hope." The long pause teared up her eyes. "Don't worry, sweetie. I've got my own personal police protection standin right here." She hung up. "My mom's run out of tranquilizers. She's takin some kick ass stuff. Ever since she saved me from that pit bull.... It's her first panic attack in six months. All of this stuff bout Serena.... Dad's still out of town, so....Gotta pick up her prescription. Comin?"

61

The glass wall that separated Rita's intensive care room from the outside world also separated Lindsey-Smith from the friend who needed to know she was not alone. Multiple tubes, life measuring and saving machines and the constant flow of masked caregivers and doctors over-shadowed the big woman whose life tilted towards death's handshake. The lady on TV with dazzling diamond stud earrings and a melted face must have looked just like Rita.

The nurse who changed Rita's urine bag approached Lindsey-Smith.

"She's in a drug induced coma to manage the pain. Otherwise, it would be more than she could bear. She's lucky. If she swallowed the hydrochloric acid she would be dead."

As the nurse receded Lindsey-Smith shot the word *lucky*.

"Bastard!" She spat. "Why her? God, why would somebody do that?" Without answering the nurse hurried to her next patient. "Lake, where the hell are you?" She leaned her head against the cool glass, dug her fists in her pockets so deep the knuckles threatened to rip through the fabric. Her right hand was practically numb, but she didn't care. For the most part it still worked—sort of.

Her phone rang. She answered it with the numb hand. From her pocket spilled tiny yellow pills. She scooped them up. "Where are you? I thought you were meetin me up here after you made the call and parked the Rover." Poor reception forced her out of ICU. "Send em. Send both photos. I need to see what the bastard looks like, now." She listened impatiently. "I can handle lookin at his pictures, come on. I need to do this. See you when you get here.

Don't you police have a doohickey you put on your cars so you don't get towed?" Stroger Hospital had a reputation for zero parking and instant towing. Lake would have to park the Rover miles away, then walk back. "Tell you what, I'll meet you outside. Stay with the Rover. They'll be kickin me out in a minute. Anyway, they've put Rita in a coma. So you can forget about talkin to her."

She shuffled back to ICU to say goodbye to Rita, possibly for the last time. One of them might not make it through the night.

The black stain on her soul spread. The murderous rage inside her comforted her. She tasted power. Rolled it around her mouth and accepted it.

62

Lindsey-Smith hurried through the hospital as she checked out a video of Rita caught on a digital camera by her bartender, Kathy, who had turned it over to the Lake. It was but a snippet. She watched it four times. Rita on fire lit it up, her rage palpable.

"How dare they ask a black woman how she came by money to do the right thing by black kids who start life with a negative balance? Poor parents. Poor schools that the accusers refuse to support with their cute money. Would you ask a white person that? No! You praise them and put them on feel good TV." Filmed in her bar Rita, her baby blues morphing between cold steel and frozen water, got in a yelling match with Gaydar hostess Prada. *"Bitch, don't you dare come up in here defendin that shit. Talkin nonsense bout you want to interview me cause I'm LS's friend. Get the hell...."* The video ended.

"That's my girl." Too late she regretted that she never made love to Rita. That was really all Rita ever wanted she reflected. More than a few times she had said, *Cheri, you got quite the smile.* Hospital smells permeated her consciousness. She found herself in front of a bank of elevators. The up and down buttons had already been punched although she was the only one standing there. In the meantime, while she waited, she found the courage, which she had denied she needed to look at Rita's attacker.

She hit the button. A head to toe shot of the man popped up.

A man, maybe in his eighties, strolled towards the camera seemingly unaware that he was being filmed. He appeared benign she noted except for that stride of his. She brought the phone closer. Yes, it was his stride—a tad too long and straight for any octogenarian. It reminded her of the quick stepping old bartender at the tavern that didn't exist. Her neck stiffened.

Rita's attacker wore a disguise. Lake had explained that the acid attack victims who survived each described a man of different ages and ethnicities, though usually the height remained consistent within inches. What are the odds of having two serials wearing disguises active at the same time in the same city Lake had asked shaking her head?

Although she knew it was impossible Lindsey-Smith tried looking past the disguise. But all she could see was white. However, the man could have been black. If you're black you know it when you see it. On the other hand, his costume appeared as old as him, yet not something typically worn by black men of any age. "Khakis and loafers?" An image that played on the fringe of her brain refused to come forward. Had she seen it before, the outfit disturbed her? White men didn't iron their khakis, on the other hand, black men were known to press sweat pants. The elevator arrived.

Snow covered the city. As far as she could see everything was covered in several inches of snow. It had not been snowing when she arrived at the hospital twenty minutes earlier. "Twenty minutes." Her feet sank into the snow. She brushed the snow from her head. If the snow got any higher it would get inside her shoes. It would be weeks before she could pull on boots without passing out from pain. So much for warm winter boots.

To the east she saw the tops of buildings disappear into a white out. Just like that the Chicago downtown skyline disappeared.

She walked up and down the front of the hospital hoping it was the snow that prevented Lake from seeing her. Parked down the block on the opposite side of the street she saw the Rover and hurried across to it.

"Lake?" She pulled the door handle. "Hey, it's locked." She could barely make out that Lake wasn't inside. "Damn it, woman!"

"Excuse me. Lieutenant Lake said to give you these." A young guard wrapped in white handed her the Rover's keys.

"She said she had to take a call. Couldn't get a signal or something" He took off running trying to dodge a blanket of falling snow leaving her staring at the keys stupidly.

Snow crowned her head as she sat behind the wheel wondering what happened to *I'm not leavin your side*. She couldn't imagine what would make Lake take off, except, just one step under breathing was stopping the 7s Killer. It had to be that. She dialed Lake. No answer and the call didn't go to message.

Three times she tried and failed. "Let's not do this." She stuck the key in the ignition just as a guard approached and waved her on.

"You can't park here."

She lowered the window. "Sir?" She didn't feel polite. "A guard just gave me my keys. I need to ask him a question about the detective who gave them to him... I mean her." Then she realized it could've been either. "An Asian."

"Asian?"

He sounded as if she had insulted him.

"Nobody work here named Asian."

"I mean like Chinese."

"Naw, none of them either. Move on. This is for pick-ups and drop-offs." He took out his ticket book.

"*She* was definitely Asian. Sir!" This time politeness turned to insult.

"I already told you." He started writing. She roared off.

Lake Michigan's blue waters lay still under a white lace curtain that extended from the sky. Traffic eased to its destination encased in igloos while pedestrians trudged like polar bears on the tundra.

The weather was alive and living and breathing.

Halloween night had come to lie under a wet white blanket; remembering slipped a shiver down her back. A drop of cold perspiration traveled from her nape down the center of her back until it met the Ace Bandage. She felt like she was going backwards.

She stuck her hand outside the window and grabbed a fist of

snow. It did little to cool down the scorching heat on the back of her hand that looked like it had touched a hot oven rack.

But that pain disappeared behind a bigger pain. "If I get out of this I'm goin after the man who did this to you." She vowed to Rita. A tear hung on the rim of her eyelid. "I'll cut off his fuckin head and bring it to you, baby. You can put one of your voodoo spells on it and fuck him up real good for eternity." The tear rolled and others followed.

The calm that followed smelled of death, chloroform.

"Khakis. LOAFERS?" She screamed so loud her head swam. The old man outside her emergency room with the aluminum cane wore pressed khakis and loafers. "And *he* was white." At least from the rear, which was the only view she had of him and that was for only an instant. Her judgment, based solely on the thin mousy brown straight hair that stuck out from under his cap and the color of the hand holding the cane, assumed things it shouldn't have. The man in the video had disguised himself in a gray wig. But it was the crease in those khakis that stayed with her. "It was him. It *is* him. Oh, my God." She hit speed dial. Lake needed to know the 7s Killer and the Acid Man and Jesus were one and the same. "C'mon, Lake. Pick up. He's here."

First the world went black. Behind her eyelids she saw red. Then the Rover ran up on the curb and slammed into a fire hydrant. It slammed home: the bartender's video clip had been used by Gaydar as a promo, which meant they had aired it over and over and the monster had probably viewed it over and over until.... The car door flung open. She threw up. An empty stomach produced bitter bile, a broken heart nearly stopped beating, and a friend's anguish pissed on her faith in God. Because Rita defended her friend the devil licked her face. "Rita Rita Rita." Her eyes fluttered open.

Color disappeared from her vision.

A stolen look in the visor mirror confirmed more. They were white, the sockets where her eyes use to be. She choked down a bunch of tranquilizers. And with an incredibly nasty taste in her mouth she announced, "Time!"

63

That extra run to the sports store for snow gear slowed JP's progress to a crawl on the freeway to freedom. His windshield wipers beat but barely stayed in front of the snow accumulating between swipes. Wind gusts stacked snow in waist high drifts indiscriminately across the roadway. Snow rode high on the thickly thatched trucks and cars.

Even stuck in snail traffic he was thankful for the unpredicted blizzard, but not for Mister-fuckin-blinkin-right-turn-signal who he had been stuck behind for the last mile. Getaways were time sensitive. In his case, he had a plane to catch at O'Hara International Airport in three hours for Amsterdam. At the moment he didn't think planes would be leaving on time. Maybe the snow didn't benefit him. For the moment, however, it did.

The artic suit he wore would camouflage him in the snowy woods. The cunt had a gun and there was no reason to feel she wouldn't use it, especially, after what he had for her ass. As usual he was prepared for everything. The car in front hit a drift. Mister Turn Signal spun his wheels deeper in a snow rut.

Stuck and enraged, JP threw the van in reverse, right smack into a vehicle behind him. It bounced and fishtailed into traffic sideswiping several cars and a pick up. The driver of the pick-up, wedged between a truck and car, jumped out and stomped through the snow to the van.

Too preoccupied with rocking the van in a failing attempt to get unstuck, JP didn't see the man coming until he smacked the driver's side window. JP lowered it and a wet cold towel smacked him across the face and fell to his chest forming a mini-cornice.

Rather than listen to the driver rail, he pulled the artic suit's hood over his head then pulled on his artic gloves.

An explosion shattered the sounds: honking horns, spinning tires, gnashing metal. Red polka dots spotted the snow. "Welcome to my hell." It felt as uplifting as his special tonic. He returned the .9mm to its hidden compartment as the van slow-poked out of there. His respiration shot up. No longer invisible he had his face back—until the next time.

In the slow lane a car plowed sideways under a Bekin Moving van.

"Welcome."

And the snow kept right on coming. Panic permeated the air. Snow hushed it.

JP exited the freeway. Visibility was reduced to a few feet. It was impossible to judge exactly where the entrance to the forest preserve was located. Two feet of sudden snow had stalled Chicagoland into a parking lot. Time ticked.

Without four-wheel drive, he realized that the van could not make the trip to the airport. Yet, that did not present a big problem, certainly not one big enough to force him to alter his perfect plan. After he finished what he came to do, he decided to take the cunt's Rover to his next destination. If he abandoned the SUV at the el station he could take the train and avoid the chaos. The el would take him right into the airport keeping time on his side and snow off his butt.

In the meantime, ahead of him two square miles of Norman Rockwell woods challenged with an overture of distant church bells tolling *O Holy Night.* Unable to eyeball the entrance to the picnic spot, JP consulted the GPS on the dashboard. It was down. He checked his left wrist. The GPS that would eventually bring her to him, it was down.

"What the…?" Now he had a problem. Without GPS the Cutter kid couldn't find him. Now what? The answer groaned in the back of the van. He giggled at his altered plan.

64

It took a nano second for Lindsey-Smith's head to wrap around what Lake was telling her. She interrupted. "You're followin him? But...but...." Lake continued speaking as if Lindsey-Smith hadn't spoken.

"He just jumped on the Eden's headed north." Lake uncharacteristically shouted.

Regrettably, that feeling of going backwards paid off as she headed in the opposite direction. Then Lindsey-Smith lost the call.

The number from which Lake had called registered as unknown name and number on caller ID. She tried callback. The number was blocked. She assumed Lake had picked up a throwaway because the FBI had ears on her BlackBerry.

Finally, she was able to make a u-turn down a residential side street where traffic flow remained light. The Rover's real deal four-wheel drive gave her an edge. Conditions considered, the SUV made good time until she was forced by a dead end to return to the main drag. Bedlam. Traffic leading to the expressway's entrance extended as far as the eye could see, which wasn't far. "Damn you." Lindsey-Smith had a thousand questions for Lake and a few things she needed to tell her. "Fat chance!" She shouted at the snow at the traffic at the stalled cars at her eye sockets that made no sense since she could see. She reasoned she should be hysterical.

A calm so calm settled her down, way down, so far down so fast it occurred to her that she might have taken too many little yellow pills. How many was too many she didn't have a clue. One left her mother ripped, that much she knew.

Nowhere fast loomed as her destination, yet it grounded

her brain and pulled her thoughts into alignment. She had to keep telling herself that as she sat dumbly in traffic.

Her phone chimed. "Lake!"

"I'm in a mcdrop zone."

She heard rustling on the other end. "How do you know it's him?"

There was a long hesitation. Lake came back uber-calm. *"His high A-sharp voice."* Another pause. Then she continued speaking, this time speaking fast. *"We just passed Old Orchard. He kidnapped Jahara. West—"*

The call was snatched out of the air.

"Jahara? He kidnapped Jahara." She was talking to dead air. "What...Jahara? Talk to me, Lake. Lake?" Technology was not her friend. Her hand resisted throwing the phone at the windshield. Instead she nearly crushed it gripping it until she felt the numbness decrease in the aching hand. The back of it, where the imprint of fingers rutted it, had begun to ooze silvery white blood fascinating her. For some odd reason clutching the phone made her feel better. Yet it weakened not strengthened her.

She un-holstered her gun and held hands with it instead.

Now the nightmare about Jahara's classmates kicking her to death made sense. At the time the clue had gone an octave above her head. Because she missed it Jahara had been kidnapped. She wanted to ask all the questions: how did he get to Jahara? Why her, a girl who didn't fit the profile? How did Lake get involved? Was that the call she took back at the hospital? Did any of it matter?

What mattered was Lake had said the word *west* before the call dropped. Out of context the word meant nothing to Lindsey-Smith. Did it mean they were going west? Couldn't be. The Eden's ran north and south. Old Orchard shopping center was east of the expressway. He wouldn't be going there. *West* made no connections. And if Lake couldn't reach her before she engaged the killer, Lindsey-Smith didn't like the question or its answer. Lake would lose. The battle with the killer was Lindsey-Smith's to win. Or lose.

Steam puffed from under the Rover's crumpled hood.

Salvation was the snowplow that scraped past. Lindsey-Smith pulled behind the plow and followed in its path. She turned on the radio ostensibly to hear the weather even though she knew it wouldn't get better. Well, if it was bad for her it was bad for the killer. The blizzard was an equalizer. She switched it off when she heard a news bulletin about multiple mysterious deaths at a State of Illinois Unemployment office.

From nowhere a song came playing across her brain. A cerebral trick twisted the lyric and altered the melody. Funeral chords mocked. James Brown shouted out the names of the murdered girls then took it to the bridge.

It was happening again. She had come full circle. Because Jahara reminded her so much of Serena she had adopted the class whose prognoses for the future were gloomy. Now, like Serena, Jahara had been snatched by a pedophile because Lindsey-Smith put her in harm's way. A long suppressed memory, taking no hostages, shot her in the head.

Her memory bank ran backwards twenty years to her family's manicured front yard lawn. Her tiny hand accepts a pretty lollipop that resembles happy Serena. The shadow of a man grabs Serena. The pretty lollipop slides from Lindsey-Smith's hand to the curb and into the sewer. Serena screams, *help me, Smithers,* as she is stuffed in the back of a big black car—the blackest car she ever saw. Mercilessly, the film looped, repeating itself over and over again.

Until now she had no memory of the part she played in getting Serena kidnapped; deep inside she always knew that it was her fault. As the film bled out memories of the lost lollipop it mingled with a little boy's memory of a lollipop, eventually melting them together, in one hot mess. Pearly tears ran from her eye sockets. She couldn't catch her breath. The world moved in and out in severe slow motion threatening to do the same to her. The pills pulled her down when she wanted to blow up. In another hour she'd be flat out, maybe sooner, what did she know? Rage wouldn't come; she knew that much. She needed its wake up call. She needed to curl up next to Serena and start life all over again. Mostly she needed to send the devil to hell with postage due.

"Forget the two head shots. That's too humane."

The fantasy about catching the man who kidnapped her little sister had long been put to sleep. Apparently it had awakened. She thought about her discussion with Rita about the degrees of separation and coming full circle.

"No more girls will die at his hands. I promise you, Serena. And this one I keep."

The Rover made no such promise. It puffed vapor, stalled and died. Lake was getting further away. The snowplow stopped. Lindsey-Smith climbed out.

Snow packed in her shoes. Gales whipped snow in her face blinding her. She drudged on until she and the snowplow operator made eye to eye contact. He stared into her sockets; the gun in her hand escaped his attention. She rapped it against the window. The shadow rubbed up against the hole in her soul. Its singed edges still burned white hot reminding her that the eyes of innocents it possessed compelled her to revenge them. Anybody who got in the way of that was disposable.

"You crazy? Git off my truck?"

She cocked the gun.

"Aight!" The operator laughed. "A pink gun—"

BANG

A bullet whizzed by his head and ricocheted around the cab.

"Get out!" Her sockets glared at him. Neon white tears produced by pelting snow oozed from the corners.

The driver jumped into a waist high snowdrift and landed face first screaming, "Take it!"

Woozy Lindsey-Smith shoved cars aside with the plow until she reached the sidewalk. Stunned pedestrians fell in snow banks to get out of the way some thanking God for answering their prayers. Those pedestrians going her way gladly followed the cleared path behind the plow. People trapped inside stores cheered and followed the leader.

Once on the freeway bumper to bumper traffic left the

plow with one option: ride the shoulder. Every half mile the plow shoved a vehicle off the shoulder demolition derby style. Lindsey-Smith ignored the pissed motorists in her wake. Her feet, now ice blocks, tingled, and squished around in her shoes making her feel alive and cold inside. She pressed on struggling with the behemoth determined to do the dyke thing: drive anything.

"Call me, Lake! C'mon, honey. I can't do it without you."

She was making good time compared to traffic. Yet that iceberg on her nape had nothing to do with blowing wind. What if Lake's replacement cell failed? She desperately needed to know what kind of time the plow was making. Was she getting closer to catching up with Lake who didn't have the advantage of the snowplow? No matter how hard she ruminated until Lake called she wouldn't know. Lake's Crown Victoria didn't have four-wheel drive. It could get stuck? There was that possibility, too. The bad possibilities were adding up with few checks and balances.

She thumbed ICU's number. Rita's status remained grave and as fate would have it Lake called while she talked with Rita's nurse.

"He's turnin into the Iroquois F. P. West—"

"Damn it." She threw the phone. Numbness in her right hand prevented her from launching it hard or far. After retrieving it she held on tight. The struggle to keep blood circulating in her hand distracted her from the finger patterns etched on the back of her chalky white hand.

"Where the hell is the Iroquois Forest Preserve?" She reflected back on the Rover with its GPS and almost wished for it. "And why the hell do you keep sayin *west?*" Ahead the signs, more like Popsicle sticks, offered no answers. She had hoped to find an exit sign for Iroquois Forest Preserve that wasn't obliterated by snow like the signs she had seen so far. "Otherwise, we're so screwed, Lake." The thought of having missed the sign could not be entertained. So she pedaled on with a brick of ice for a foot. "*A*-sharp? She said, '*A*-sharp'. Lake, you're tone deaf. How would you know....?" Her voice trailed. The better question broke the sound barrier: when and where did Lake encounter the bastard and his voice? No answer to that could be good. About to dismiss the thought she doubled back. "No way. My poor baby wouldn't know an A...." Her voiced trailed until it found its bottom. "Lake, no! NOOO!" She broke into a million pieces.

The killer had Lake.

When Lindsey-Smith asked Lake how she identified the killer Lake had hesitated too long as if she needed to think about it. At the time it didn't resonate. Now it thundered. She dipped into the right lane. "Bastard's disconnectin her every time she says *west*. So if *west* is a clue, what're you tryin to tell me, Lake?" Her nose twitched. Without GPS, or a map she had a problem. No, they had a problem. There had to be a forest preserve west of the mall. The pervert had GPS and she had nothin. "Call me, prick. I'm onto you. Just gemme the go'damn directions. I know what you're doin. It aint gonna work."

But it was working. He was way ahead of her and had been since the *Gaydar* interview. Realization bit her on the bottom lip; while she thought she was setting him up he had managed to set her up. He had not worn the wristband GPS so that it would come down to him directing her into his trap. Her mouth continued to chatter afraid that if it didn't move the tranquilizers would impede her reasoning.

Steel scraped against concrete. The insanity of the white humped world that she struggled to survive in felt like the noise beneath her. Both wanted to crush her, but to her it was rock and roll. And she had a lyric to fit it; her mouth sang: *Get out of my lane.*

In spite of playing badass, white neon pearls flowed from white eye sockets down her face and dripped onto her coat leaving glowing trails against the nappy wool of her life. She put women in her life in harm's way: her mother, her baby sister, her lover, "Jahara." The whispered name smothered her pity party. The complaining world that got in her way ceased to exist. Lindsey-Smith heard the wind howling. She saw white. She sensed cold. She felt the 7s Killer's Adam's apple beneath her crushing thumbs and squeezed the phone until it cracked. "On God's name." She vowed. It was almost more than she could stand. Just when she thought she couldn't take it anymore, her insides went as cold as her feet when a car blocked the plow; its door swung open.

Lindsey-Smith slammed on the brakes and shifted gears. The plow ground to a stop. She rolled the window down. "Move it or lose it!" The palace blue blinking roof rack shone through the snow. "Cops." She wanted no part of them.

A woman shouted, "Chicago PD. Put your left hand outside the window. Reach outside with your right hand and open the door."

"Can't reach it." She yelled. "I can't reach it from here." The plow's cab wasn't a car. That move was impossible, especially with broken ribs. "This thing must have LoJack."

"Let me see your hands! Now!"

"Okay."

"Show me your go'damn hands now!"

"They're hangin out the window." It became obvious that, like her, the officers couldn't see beyond two feet in front of them.

"Get out of there. Step out the vehicle."

Although her lazy eyes could barely make out the officer's gun, she knew it had to be pointed at her. The driver's side door yawned opened.

Lindsey-Smith had choices. Get arrested and it was over for Lake and Jahara. Shoot the cop and they lived. She fired. The bullet slammed into the police officer knocking the woman backward. Before the other officer could recover the plow truck rammed the cruiser. He recovered. Something slammed into her thigh.

White flowed from her thigh in a silvery stream down her leg.

65

Connors stood with his back to the door looking out the window at the debacle on Elston Avenue confident that neither the 7s Killer or the Acid Man would cause him trouble today. At least he could relax knowing nothing would happen during a blizzard of biblical proportions.

He didn't hear the door open. But he heard a throat being cleared. Startled, he pivoted around ready to cut the interloper down for not knocking before entering. Instead he stepped back as if he'd been hit. And then he was—slapped.

Arm in a sling, Chief Boggs stood next to Superintendent Smith. Two FBI agents strolled in behind them.

"Chief Boggs!" His voice cracked. "You...you...you're alive."

"You're under arrest." Chief Boggs said dead calm.

"What...what're you...whacha mean I'm under arrest? Nonsense." The FBI agents handcuffed him roughly. "Git off!"

"We have evidence that you hired Papa John Kent to kill me."

"You're not gettin off like John Birges." The super charged.

"It was a long time ago. But you must have figured out the eye witness was me."

"Your ex-partner confided in you that a secret grand jury was bein convened involvin a murder you were called out on as a rookie." Smith added. "Never liked you."

"I was a rookie, too, back then. I didn't realize until recently what I saw. Thanks to something your arrogance made you say. You killed that man. And ripped him off. Gold coins worth millions that *I* never saw at the scene. And you sold em." She pulled a photograph out of her sling and shoved it in his face as the fibbers marched him to the door. "Your buyer ID'd you when they picked him up four months ago tryin to auction em off. Stupid, after all these years you sold em thinkin the insurers forget, maybe. Greedy stupid man."

West cocked his head, "Chief, Mista High IQ put an APB on Lindsey-Smith Cutter. He just added armed and dangerous. She's a target out there."

"She shot a cop." Connors screamed as he was led out.

"It hit her vest. Trust me, chief. Aint no time to explain. Ah just got a call from her. Lake and a girl named Jahara been snatched by the serial."

Her eyebrows shot up. "The 7s Killer? Did I just call him…? Go on, West."

"The girl's missin fo sho. Her parents just verified it. And Ah caint reach Lieu."

Boggs picked up the phone and called off the APB as the two men began putting a plan together.

"Iroquois." West pronounced the *s*. He hurried through it, "That's all Lieu told her before bein cutoff. All them woods he killed in had them sillybents, just like the girls' names. Cept Jahara don't. Uh uhhh." He took a breath. "Welcome back, Chief."

"Sorry I couldn't bring you in on it." She looked out the window and shook her head in disgust at the snow. "That's a problem."

"Did Lieu know you were alive?" His face drooped.

"She was ordered to keep an eye on Connors. Yes." Superintendent Smith put the phone on speaker. After a minute of fierce negotiation he announced, "Let's go get em."

"There's a white out. Chopper aint gonna fly." West pointed at the phone as if the speaker was still objecting.

"It can and it will." The Chief said exiting her office.

66

The forest wore its white down blankets like royal woodies, which she saw sticking up from the freeway and went for it. If it meant checking every forest preserve off the Edens, then so be it.

"How do you expect me to find you without directions? Whatcha up to? Watch out for the trap, girlfriend. Of course, there's a trap." Thoughts floated off with the little yellow pills. "Focus!"

Her world may have been shades of white, but she saw clearly those shades of white. A van parked in a lot lay like a humpback whale interrupting the tree line. She plowed in. Lazy eyes slung down and peered at the tourniquet, the Ace Bandage, around her thigh. It had cut off circulation. The plow pushed into the woods snapping and bowing trees until they were too thick and too close for her to continue. She disembarked clumsily. Her right thigh and leg were completely encased in liquid silver that squished in her shoe when she landed in the snow. Where blood spilled the snow turn tarnished silver. It finally registered, she felt no pain, not even from the gunshot, yet she couldn't recall when she became pain free.

As she bent over to loosen the tourniquet she heard a shot, felt the impact but not the pain when the bullet creased her scalp. In the distance, a body, unmoving stood between two trees behind a waist high snow bank. She saw it clearly with 20-20 that spied white smoke rising from a gun in the body's hand.

BANG BANG

JP spun around stunned that she could see him. His shoulder exploded in pain. Blood sprouted. Snow around him turned red.

He struggled to his knees, and then to his feet as he searched the distance for the cunt's body. If his gun hadn't been hot he wouldn't have found it in the snow. He adjusted his goggles.

Because of flan legs, Lindsey-Smith stroked her way belly down through the snow towards the fleeing white figure stomping its way among trees. It had been at least an hour since she took the clonazepam. They weren't through taking her down. Her body had a dilemma. It could snuff her out with the pills or bleed out before she did what she needed to do. Every weakening stroke reminded her not to give death its head until her job on earth was complete, and then she could go to hell.

"How bout that? I killed myself." She gulped mouthfuls of snow preventing her body from shutting down grounding herself with a mantra, "Double tap headshot." Her thoughts went loosey-goosey. It was time to call Detective West. She touched her pocket and whimpered. The phone must have fallen out when the shot knocked her down. She plowed on. "Double tap head shot."

Tracks splattered with arctic silver led to her left. The blizzard busied itself with covering the bloody white trail, yet the white shadow moving among the trees remained crystal clear. Now she understood the reason for her new eyes.

In the back of her mind she saw the blue snake slither up the legless man's nose. She didn't even want to imagine what death would be like if she failed, which is exactly what would happen if she didn't get on her feet. "Get off your belly, be'atch." Stomping through the snow on one leg, she dragged the other behind her. The head wound like all head wounds bled profusely coating half her face. Blood went in a circle her oxygen deprived brain mocked. Looky looky, he lost. Where his GPS? Trap. Trap! See trap. Run. In a race with unconsciousness she was loosing.

Forward she lurched doing her best mummy imitation.

"You bastard, you can't bust a nut without me. I'm the party."

Blood dripped from JP into Lake's face as he turned over her bound body laying face down in the snow. "Get up, cunt. The chloroform's wearin off. You aint foolin nobody. Get up!" He kicked her in the stomach. "Smithers, throw away your gun. Unless you want a dead pussy before you say your goodbyes." He put the gun to Jahara's head.

"He's gonna shoot the baby." Lake slurred.

"I'm gonna kill you, you stupid fuck." In her numb hand pinky took a shaky aim at JP's head.

Under the tallest tree, in the clearing, Lake's distinctive panther-like silhouette packed in the white stuff stood out against the forest background. She shivered uncontrollably; Lindsey-Smith read her body language—fear.

"You want Serena? Here she is." JP stood behind Jahara. She heard him cock his big ol gun. Lindsey-Smith dropped the silver blood soaked 9mm. It sunk out of view leaving a silver streak in its decent.

"That was too easy. You're up to something. Take off your clothes. You got another gun? Do you carry two like your cunt over here?"

His high voice made her ears bleed, which kept a small part of her, the ears, alert.

"I said take em off and fling them towards me. I wanna see em." Lindsey-Smith took off her coat, and then her top. "Turn round slow."

She complied. Her head tilted forward. Who's he kidding he can't see anything. She still had on an undershirt and he didn't continue to object. Her knees wobbled. She needed a plan. Fast. She was on her way out.

"This little bitch could be Serena's twin."

"Shut up. Shut UP!"

"You took candy from a stranger. Smart kid." Jahara held out something to Lindsey-Smith. "She's got a button from Serena's little sailor's dress. It's shaped like a sail boat. Found it where you're standin. Right there. Maybe you're standin on a piece of her. Imagine a critter draggin a piece of her over there cause I broke her neck over here."

"SHUT UP!" The yelling sent her rage into a swoon. Where

was the plan? Her knees buckled. Not that plan. Lindsey-Smith swayed badly. She felt herself dying. Her body shifted downward. Silver streaks covered her face, flowed in her eyes. Her hand went totally numb again. Her body followed.

"That's right, baby. Don't listen to him. Don't list...." JP slapped Lake across the mouth with his gun. She went down softly, without a sound and disappeared in a snow drift.

Lindsey-Smith whimpered.

JP's head jockeyed side to side as he strained to see her across the clearing through snow swirling down on them at tornadic speed. Her weight shifted forward. He didn't react because he couldn't see her. She knew it and she couldn't take advantage of it.

"Red white and blue buttons on a white sailor dress, you remember the dress she wore that day don't you? Maybe there're more bones round here somewhere, you think?" His wicked voice mimicked the last thing she heard Serena say, "'Smithers, help me. Help—'"

A scream from Serena's big sister cut him off. "Sereeenaaa!" Her subconscious could suppress the images no longer: Serena's body beneath JP's, her face among his collection, *Suzy, Sally, Betsey, Serena....* Serena's neck snapped in Lindsey-Smith's hands, in his, in her hands; in her tiny hand the lollipop; in situ, in all the girls' hands he placed the melted lollipop from the mountain top. One clue. She had asked the legless man for one clue. And then suppressed it for it had been more than she could handle.

Lindsey-Smith pitched forward on her face.

Lake screamed. "You killed her."

"Get the fuck up, cunt! Don't play me. I'll kill this little rich bitch." He grabbed Jahara by the throat, "Serena gonna dieee." He fired watching Lindsey-Smith's body for movement. "Cunt!" Instead, the sight of a spreading red patch shriveled his cock. He hadn't meant to kill her so soon. To be sure he aimed at Lake's throat. "I'll blow your woman away. Get up! Go'damn you. You're not dead till I say you're dead. Her death is on you."

Although she could see only snow, Lake refused to look away from the spot where Lindsey-Smith lay.

BANG BANG

Amazed, JP looked down slowly at the sixth inch hole where his crotch used to be. He crumbled.

Lindsey-Smith mumbled, "Double tap head...." Pinky slipped from her hand. In its place she felt a small delicate hand. She squeezed back. From far away an unfamiliar voice welcomed her with the words *I love you*. She smiled as suffocating blackness claimed her.

Howling wind cried wolf creating swirling snow that lifted two bodies and every snow crystal in the woods. The blizzard ceased, dropping the bodies, one twisted into a pretzel, on the forest floor.

Air swirled as paramedics jumped out of the police chopper ahead of Chief Boggs and West and went to work on Lindsey-Smith. They worked forever.

"Call it!" A paramedic ordered.

"She's not dead. Don't stop!" Lake took Lindsey-Smith's limp hand in hers and felt for the fight her woman possessed. Jahara knelt and prayed.

A grand cosmic symphony produced by colliding celestial bodies struck up a fanfare. At the rim of forever Jass faltered before Satan. His aroused arrows pointed towards her. The hand that she could not see, she crushed it, refused to release it even as she drained its strength. The knowledge that she had taken too much in order to survive almost undid her will to resist Satan's offer for she had her wish. Her knight in shinning armor, just like in the childhood stories where in the face of peril she found love for eternity in her woman's arms, had reached out and saved her from falling. "I love you." She whispered gratefully.

"Come kiss your pussy's destiny. Inside out, ba-bee." Satan threw her a kiss. By her head he snatched her across the black hole.

"You're okay, baby. They can't hurt you. I love you, too,

Jass. You're safe now. You're in the hospital." Crystal Bernea realized that she held her daughter's hand a tad too tight.

XXXX

An hour later as Crystal drove down PCH she felt the stirrings of her childhood. Unfortunately, at the end of the reflection her father wouldn't be there to make everything perfect again. She was and would always be daddy's girl just like her sixteen-year-old daughter. But their fathers were deceased. Neither woman ever forgave them for dying.

Nor would she have been able to forgive her child if she had died. "Honey, who would want to murder you, and why? Were you talkin out of your head?" Her child had pleaded, *Dracula killed me. You promised to always believe me. You promised.*

Dracula, the medic had informed Crystal, arrived at the morgue with a black Mercedes wrapped around his hips. It was after all, Halloween. Who was she to believe her levelheaded daughter or the lying circumstances?

She needed to see Dracula's body.

It wouldn't be easy to look at a crushed human, yet she was compelled to do it. She had to see who or what terrorized her child. The gore be damned. She would do anything to protect her Jass.

Off the highway Crystal saw a hole-in-the-wall. Without a second thought she turned into an unpaved parking lot. Pebbles pinged against the undercarriage of her hybrid.

The door opened with barely a touch from her. The thought of turning back slipped around the surface of her brain. The place smelled of rotgut booze, stale smoke, and old man funk. All the occupants she noted were old.

She saw one empty stool.

To its right a shriveled old stud beckoned the woman to come and sit next to her. At first hesitant Crystal decided she needed a drink. The old thing pointed to a wall clock behind the bar.

"Halloween aint over." The old thing crowed. "Which one are you, the fox or the hedgehog?"

"Trick or treat." Crystal snapped.

-TO BE CONTINUED-

Read the next episode in the series *Be Careful of What You Wish 4* in the case of *The Fox and Hedgehog.*

About the Author

Barbara J. Wells runs a mystery storyline through all creative projects including her participatory children's plays and one of a kind handsewn leather bags. She believes until science solves it all things are a mystery. An avid reader of mysteries she lives in the Chicagoland area. To download novel's music contact her at becarefulofwhatyouwish4@gmail.com